Love Mammy
(Emails from an Irish Mother)

Helen Leahy

For my own Mammy and Daddy May and Denis
Leahy.
Thanks for everything.

ACKNOWLEDGEMENTS

I would like to thank all the people who have read this book from it's infancy and whose encouragement have kept me going during times of doubt. These include my sisters; Kay Durose, Marie McCarthy, Paula Leahy Watson and Deirdre Goode. My dear friend Tina Jhalli, my neighbours and friends Theresa, Ted, William and the girls. My nieces Kerry Durose, Shauanna Lee Lynch, May Watson and my nephews Terry, Denis and Gary McCarthy, Paul Durose and Eoin Leahy. I would also like to mention my brother Pearse Leahy and my almost brother Timmy Ryall who gave me permission to base Timmy (very loosely) on him.
Thanks to Mark Robbins for the cover illustration.
I also want to mention my darling grandchildren Jacy, Christian and Jenny who can always bring a smile to my face.
Thanks also to all the writers on Youwriteon.com and Authonomy.com for all the fantastic reviews.

To: Deirdre@aol.com
Cc: Pearse@hotmail.com; Kay@hotmail.com;
From: Mammy@ eirecom.ie
January 4th

Dear Deirdre

I opened up my mailbox today and am sure that you must have forgot to press the send button as there was no mail from you to let us know you got home safely this morning. Don't worry now at all about sending Thank You cards as family is family and we don't expect that kind of thing. If Gary wants to he can as obviously he was a guest.

It was lovely to have you home for the holidays but I must admit that the house was a bit of a mess after ye and it's taken me all day to tidy it. It's a pity now that you could not stay a bit longer as your father and I are getting older and you never know how long we will be around. Especially with my health the way it is.

I overheard you talking with Gary about your summer holidays in Brighton but hopefully you will change your mind and come home instead. What do you want to go to Brighton for anyway when you have a lovely country of your own to come to and although you didn't offer, we would never take a penny for your keep while you are here. Shur we don't mind at all buying all that fancy food from Marks & Spencers, although Daddy and I usually make do with Dunnes Stores for our groceries. I

4

did mention to your sisters and brothers that Gary has a preference for English food and that it is hardly your fault. I mentioned it to your Aunts and Uncles as well, oh and your cousins. I mentioned it only because yourself and Gary might want to visit one of them when you come for your summer holidays and it would be a shame if they didn't have any ginger chicken with lemon honey in for his sandwiches. A bit of ham or cheese usually does us with a bit of salad if it's going.

As you all know Tina, Mrs Donahague's girl was home from the US for the holidays and left €500 in a lovely thank you card hidden under her pillow. But as you know Tina's hubby is something on Wall Street and money is no object. Tina doesn't even have to work and spends all day at the gym/salon/shopping. I said to Daddy that it was lucky that Mr's D found the money at all as Tina had changed the bed linen and cleaned her room from top to bottom before she left for Cork airport at 7 o'clock yesterday morning.

I found one of Gary's dirty socks under the bed when I was cleaning the spare room this morning. Do you want me to send it on? If yes, send a stamped, addressed envelope.

Mrs D said that she didn't have to lift a finger over the whole holiday. Tina and her stockbroker husband took them out for meals and they stayed in a hotel over Xmas itself. I said to Mrs D, I didn't mind at all cooking for five of my own, 3 of their partners, 4 of their children and Daddy and myself on Xmas day and the next two days as well. My blood pressure was not that high.

When does Gary finish his studies, it's been three years now since you met him and he's never had a job apart from the band which is no job at all. I'm sure his degree in Media studies will be very useful but I do think he's a bit too old to be an MTV presenter. Aren't they usually youngish and attractive in appearance? Gary reminds me of Jack Black. Are they related?

It's a pity your sister could not get over from NY for the holidays. But I suppose she has to think of her career and I suppose that someone has to be at the hospital over the holidays. I always thought it would be lovely to have a doctor in the family, but what use is it really if she's in New York? I don't know why she can't move home, there are plenty of sick people in Cork and it would be very handy when Daddy or myself are sick as she would be able to treat us for nothing instead of us having to pay medical insurance and pay for the doctor and prescriptions. Daddy is livid because his medical insurance payments are going up again this year. He told me that I am not to go to the doctor's anymore when I get one of my heads. I can't believe the man. I know well from Kay's old medical books that a headache can be the sign of a brain tumour and it's far safer to have the brain scan than not. I'm sure you'll agree.

We might come over to London (if God spares us) when Gary starts working and you get a bigger place with double glazing and a bath. Daddy would not like to sleep on a futon at all and he might slip in the shower. I'd only go if you can assure me that I would not be mugged by the Yardies.

Are there any nice young Irish male teachers at your school?

Well I have to go now as I have an appointment at the Doctor's. He only went back to work today after the holidays. Isn't that lovely, if we had been sick over the holidays the Doctor was off in Venezuela doing God knows what.

Love Mammy.

To: Kay@hotmail.com
Cc: Deirdre@aol.com;   Pearse@hotmail.com
From: Mammy@ eirecom.ie
January 10th

Dear Dr Solomon

I get a great kick out of writing that and I'm sure you laugh every time you read it, your own mother calling you Doctor.

Well it's all back to normal here. D is gone back to London, Pearse back to Australia, Xavier is up in his room, studying I expect. Although he could be playing on the PS3 that I got him for his Xmas stocking. I have no idea where Marie is, she must have went out early this morning. I'll be glad when she is back at school; God alone knows where she is.

Daddy is having a snooze as he said he didn't get much sleep sharing the bed with Gary over the holidays. I'm sure Deirdre was expecting me to let them share the spare room but I soon put a stop to her gallop. I told her she was sleeping with me and Gary and Xavier were sleeping in Xavier's room. Well for some reason Deirdre found that very funny but Gary refused point blank to share Xavier's room. The English are very strange like that although they have no qualms about living in sin. In the end Gary and Daddy had to share the single bed in the spare room. Poor Daddy was in shock the first night because Gary got in bed wearing nothing but his underwear (bikini briefs from what I can make out). As you know Daddy was in the army for 21 years and he'd never seen the likes of that. Daddy came down and slept on the couch but he was sweating from the plastic covering. He wanted me to take the covering off but I would not. That couch is only five years old and Paul's kids can be dirty pups at times. In any case Daddy ended up sweating every night anyway as he had to wear his track suit under his pyjamas just in case Gary started any funny business. You know them fellas in bands, 'any port in a storm'. I said to Daddy 'don't you be getting any funny ideas now about coming to bed in your underwear', he said he won't. Daddy wears y-fronts not bikini briefs, I know that from doing the washing. Xavier wears things that are only held together by bits of string, he'll be freezing if it snows.

Poor Xavier was very disappointed about the sleeping arrangements as he had got his bedroom all ready for Gary with lovely matching pillowcases and scented candles. Xavier has a queen-size bed as he is a restless sleeper. I suppose he was looking forward to talking about football and hurling with Gary. To be honest I don't know why Gary had to come. You would think he would go home to his own family for Xmas.

How are you and my lovely son-in-law the surgeon? I wouldn't have to ask if you'd had the chance to write over the holidays. Tell Jerry that I said that next year he should do all his operations before Xmas and then ye could come home for the holidays. I would have thought people wouldn't be bothered with plastic surgery over the holidays. I know him being a Jew he might not like coming to midnight Mass but you never know it might make him convert. If he did convert then ye could get married properly in your own parish church and the kids could be Catholic from the start instead of having to wait to decide themselves when they are old enough. Can they still make their Holy Communion without being Catholic? That's always assuming that ye have kids. You've been married, in the eyes of the American state, for three years now and still no baby news. Do you think it could be something to do with Jerry? I assume he's circumcised and you don't what damage that can do.

Gary was supposed to come to midnight Mass but he went out to the pub with your cousin Timmy and drank 23 pints of Guinness and some stuff that you set on fire. While Timmy was drinking the stuff that was on fire he caught his hair alight and caused a big commotion in the pub and the Gardai took them to the station to sober up and did not let them out till 5 o'clock on Xmas morning. They rang here asking Daddy to collect them but I told them to walk home. Timmy came in for a cup of tea (wait till I send you the photos of his hair), and ended up drinking half a bottle of Paddy and fell asleep on the couch. He woke up and vomited but luckily the plastic covering protected the couch and it wasn't such a bad job for Daddy to clean up. The Garda told Daddy after that Gary was a bad influence on Timmy. After all Timmy had never been arrested on a Xmas eve before. His mother was raging and was threatening to come down and have a word with Gary but Timmy was too drunk to drive and Daddy would not go up to get her. I blame Gary. Drinking stuff that you set on fire, and letting children choose their religion, no wonder the world is the way it is.

Daddy said we should go over to visit you but I would be afraid of being mugged by the Bloods or Crypts.
Love Mammy.

To: Deirdre@aol.com
Cc: Pearse@hotmail.com; Kay@hotmail.com;
From: Mammy@ eirecom.ie
January 15th

Dear Deirdre

Thanks for your briefest of notes letting me know you got back safely. Glad to hear everything is fine with you.

You forgot to ask me about my visit to the Doctor's. Well I got a shock when I got there as Dr Nolan wasn't there although I could have sworn I saw him running past the reception. Anyway there was another Doctor there instead and he was quite rude. He told me that the fact that my nails were breaking was not a sign of Brittle Bone disease (although I'm sure I read it was). He absolutely refused point blank to send me for a bone scan so God alone knows what condition my bones are in. I went out and told your father to go in and have a word with him but your father said no, he would not. I was going to ring Paul to come down in his uniform and frighten the life out of the doctor but that receptionist said the Doctor had left and they were closing for the day. I pointed out that it was only 5 o'clock but she said that it was holiday hours. I made another appointment for next week when Doctor Nolan will be back. I can only hope that my skeleton does not collapse before then.

Daddy told me he had a surprise for me. I thought it was something to do with a beautiful pink diamond ring I had pointed out to him down the Grand Parade, but no. Daddy said that he had retired too young and had got a new job being a courier. I said I hoped he wasn't smuggling drugs. He said no, he wasn't. I asked him what a courier did and he said he would be taking things up to Dublin on the train a few times a week and getting paid for it. I said would they pay for his tickets and he said yes they would give him a pass. I said will they give me a pass too. He said no, the pass he got *could* be used for two tickets but without thinking he had already put Timmy's name on it and he was not allowed to change it until the pass ran out in ten years time or when he left the job, whichever came first. He said he didn't put me on the pass as I would be busy going to the Doctors and for X-rays and other medical things. I said to him that's all fine and good but how will I get to and from wherever I have to go. After all I don't want to be planning my schedule around his *job*. He said Xavier had nothing else to do so he could take me in the car I bought him for his birthday. I pointed out that Xavier is very busy studying but Daddy said that perhaps he should wait to be accepted at a college or university before he began studying in the first place. The cheek of him, as if Xavier would go to a college. I think there's a bit of jealousy there. You see Daddy wanted to spend money on a re-union holiday with

his ex-army buddies and their wives in Florida this year but I felt that the money was better spent as a deposit on a little car for Xavier. After all how would Xavier get to and from any university with no transport. Xavier had his heart set on a Mercedes sports car with a drop-top, whatever that is, and although it was a bit more than I had hoped to spend, Daddy will have it paid off in ten years time. It was worth it to see Xavier's little face light up. He said he is going to take me for a spin to Blarney when he learns to drive. Of course Daddy was complaining again when Xavier said that he didn't want the car to be robbed or damaged in front of the house and I said that Daddy would not mind parking on the road and putting the Mercedes in the garage. I really don't understand your father; his car did not cost a portion of what Xavier's cost and it does not have a drop-top.
Love Mammy

To: Kay@hotmail.com
Cc: Deirdre@aol.com ; Pearse@hotmail.com
From: Mammy@ eirecom
January 20th

Dear Doctor Solomon (Ha-ha)
I am rather disappointed that I have not heard a
word from you since your quick phone-call on New
Year's Eve. I know you are very busy doing
medical things but a little email would take you no
time at all. I did get an email from Deirdre; she's
very conscientious like that. She knows from day-
to-day whether or not her mother is alive.

Your brother's wife is expecting again. I said to
Paul 'is she ever going to stop having babies, four
is more than enough for anyone'. He said he
wasn't sure. You'd think she'd have more sense,
being a Ban Garda. I had bought Paul condoms
for Xmas but it was already too late by then. I
hope this one will have a nice colour hair now.
Blond or black, not ginger again. They are all the
image of their mother. Our Paul is a very good-
looking boy like so hopefully this one will look like
him.

I am starting a course next month. It's
Psychology for Beginners. I'd say I'd be great at
that sort of thing as I am a people person, popular
with everyone from pauper to prince. Daddy is
doing a cookery course on the same night. I don't
why he's doing cookery as he's never boiled a
kettle in his life.

Daddy wants us to go to Italy on a holiday. I said 'what kind of holiday would that be, I see you every day of my life as it is, I'm sure you'd look no different at all in Italy'. He said he might go with Timmy and Marie so. I said do. I couldn't go to Italy, I'd get mugged by the Mafia.

Myself and Mrs Donoghue and Xavier are going to see Daniel O' Dolan tomorrow night. He's a great entertainer; I don't know how some talent scout hasn't taken him to America. Although I suppose he's a bit old now to be travelling away from home (he'll be 80 this year). And who would look after his mammy? I don't know who looks after her when he's out entertaining. He used to always bring her with him and sit her in a chair on the side of the stage but I haven't seen her for a while now. Maybe she'll be there tomorrow night, I'll let you know. Xavier will be dancing all night like a mad thing.
Love Mammy

To: Pearse@hotmail.com
Cc: Deirdre@aol.com ; Kay@hotmail.com;
From: Mammy@ eirecom.ie
January 27th

Hello My Darling Boy.
I was expecting an email from you on the 5th but
don't worry at all, I know how busy you are out
there keeping Australia safe for the British ex-
con's descendants. Not forgetting the
descendants of all those poor falsely accused Irish
deportees.

Xmas was grand but I am very lonely now
without ye all at home. Although it's nice to have
the sleeping arrangements back to normal. Your
girlfriend is Chinese, did you notice that? Is she
Catholic? Will you be getting married soon? If yes
where will you get married? Would you come
home to Cork to get married that would be grand.
I hope she doesn't want to get married in China as
I couldn't go to China. I might be mugged by the
Triads. If ye moved over here she could get a job
in the Chinese chipper down Blackpool, they are
always looking for people.

I was saying to Daddy last night isn't it great
that yourself and Paul are both policemen.
Although Paul is here in Ireland keeping the Irish
people safe. Still I suppose the Australians need
policemen too, being as you could hardly trust one
of them as they are all descended from ex-cons,
except the poor Irish deportees. Still though you'd

think they'd have enough Australians to choose from.

Now Pearse take heed of your mother and be very careful on the streets out there. Don't take on any cases involving drugs, gangs, the Mafia, terrorists, assault with deadly weapons, gun-running, the Triads, the Russian Mafia, Yardies, hip-hop wars, sexual crimes, serial killers, white supremacists, the Bloods, the Crypts, (the Bloods and the Crypts have gone international now), vice or armed robbers. Just get involved in nice crimes like art fraud or un-armed robberies, but only when they are big news likely to get in the paper, you know crimes that involve hauls over $1m. White collar crime really. Don't get involved in domestics as they can easily escalate to hostage situations. I know an awful lot about police work, I do have two sons in the business. If your boss has a problem with my advice give me his phone number and I will speak to him myself. It would have to be after 6 as it's too expensive to phone during the day.

I went to see Daniel O' Dolan the other night. We had a ball. As you know I don't drink at all but Xavier had a lovely creamy drink with umbrellas and fruit and I tasted it and liked it so he got me one.

It was only after I drank fifteen of them that he told me they were laced with vodka and Malibu. Still I was grand but have a bit of an aul head today.
Xavier is a fierce laugh.
Love Mammy

To: Deirdre@aol.com
Cc: Pearse@hotmail.com ; Kay@hotmail.com;
From: Mammy@ eirecom.ie
February 4th

Dear Deirdre

Have you heard anything at all from Dr Solomon?
I have not heard a word since New Year's Eve.
Not that I've heard much from any of ye this year.

Xavier said to tell you he will be over Friday
week. He is arriving at 6 am and I told him that
yourself or Gary will pick him up from Gatwick as
he can't be wasting money on taxis. After all he is
on the dole. I gave him €500 but he wants to buy
D&G sunglasses for his holiday in Malibu with that.
Don't forget now that he can only drink bottled
water as the water in London is re-cycled about 45
times, filthy habits. Also ensure you switch on his
electric blanket 1 hour before his bedtime. Make
sure you have whitening toothpaste in for him.
Not cheap stuff now, he has sensitive gums.

He told me last time he was over you made him
smoke outside and he nearly got a cold. This time
now let him smoke inside, you can always open all
the windows and air the place out once he comes
home. It won't take five minutes, with the size of
that place. Oh he is bringing his little friend
Jeremy with him.

Jeremy is a vegan since yesterday so make sure you have loads of vegetables in. If ye have any leather stuff hide it, although I don't know what ye can do with the leather sofa, era tell him it's plastic, although I have no idea if vegans agree with plastic or not. Just a word of warning there for you now; ye would not want to insult his sensibilities. I am sending you €20 over for Xavier's keep. If you want money for Jeremy's keep you would have to ring his mother.

I'm surprised that you think Daddy getting a job is a good idea. You know I need him at home so I can get around a bit. Paul's on duty a lot and can only take me around now and then. Daddy being retired was ideal as he was there all the time. Well I suppose I will have to use taxis now, at least his wages will pay for them so that's something. I wouldn't dream of going on the bus I would get mugged by boot-boys.

I have to tell you something now that you will not like to hear. Once I start my psychology course I may not be able to email so often as I will have to devote myself to my studies. In any case I can't be writing all the time, I do have other things to do. It's grand for you being a teacher and only working a few hours a day.

Oh by the way I know you are awaiting news of my appointment with the Doctor but that

receptionist rang last week and said the Dr Nolan
is not well so I would have to see that brazen fella
I saw last time. I said no thanks so am ringing
next week to check on whether Dr Nolan is back
or not. Will keep you informed.
Love Mammy

To: Deirdre@aol.com
From: Mammy@ eirecom.ie
February 11th

Dear Deirdre

I am rather shocked that you felt that picking Xavier and Jeremy up from Gatwick tomorrow will make you late for work. I clearly said either you or Gary, I did not say that it had to be you specifically. Where would we be if Daddy took that attitude about picking you and Gary up from Cork Airport every time you come over? Surely Gary can miss a morning from his Media studies; Xavier is after all your brother. Media studies is hardly Rocket Science, I'd say all they do all day is watch tele and listen to the radio. He could do that in the car on the way there, the radio part anyway. If he does have a television in the car, tell him not to watch it while he is driving Xavier. Will his auditioning for Big Brother in the afternoon not take valuable time away from his Media Studies also?

I really hope that you were joking when you said that he is thinking of going on that show. Although I have never watched Big Brother, I know it's 'bottom of the barrel' television. We will be disgraced if Gary goes on there (and according to Daddy, Gary's underwear is no pretty sight). They all walk around half-naked the whole time. Then they have to do 'tasks' that any self-respecting person would quail from doing. At least one couple have to have a 'relationship' – shacking up would be a better description. Of course there is always a token homosexual. Now, think about this, some of the young ones who go in are very attractive and very free with sexual favours so what if Gary and one of them were the couple who had to have the relationship? Where would that leave you? It might be no bad thing though for his television presenting career – the publicity. If you really want to keep him you should consider blonde highlights and a bit of fake-tan. Also you could use the whitening toothpaste that's left over when Xavier comes home.   If he, Gary not Xavier,(Xavier has more respect for himself), does run off with some glamour model you are to come straight home and teach Irish children. After all it was the Irish taxpayer who paid for your training.

Phone me up the minute Xavier arrives safely in the morning and we can have a nice chat about how his travelling experience went.

Did I mention that the lads are going to see Madonna on Sat night.   That is the reason they are going in the first place. Luckily I managed to find tickets on E-Bay for them. I bought them for a surprise as Xavier was a bit down because he had a spray-tan that went orange.

Make sure you have a non-bio detergent for Xavier's smalls. Anything harsh gives him a rash.

It would be best if you hand washed his smalls in Lux Flakes, then soak them in a fabric softener, put them in a scented pillowcase and then tumble-dry with a fabric softening sheet, that's what I do thereby ensuring that his sensitive skin is protected.
Love Mammy

To: Deirdre@aol.com
Cc: Pearse@hotmail.com ; Kay@hotmail.com;
From: Mammy@ eirecom.ie
February 12th

Dear Deirdre

I was surprised to see a reply so quickly from you but when I read it I was quite hurt. I have been up since 4 packing Xavier's stuff so I am rather tired. However, I won't rest till you ring to say Xavier got there safely and I can have a quick word with him. Daddy was up very early too as he had to pick Jeremy up first to come down for his breakfast and then take them to the airport. It was snowing heavily and Daddy slipped when he was carrying out the lads' luggage. He said he hurt his ankle but I said to take them to the airport and if it's still hurting call into the hospital on the way back. He's not home now yet so I don't know how he went on.

Well D, I am sure you'd have loved to have gone to see Madonna and I don't know why you didn't get tickets over there in London. I would have liked to go myself, as you know I went to see her in the 80's and I would like to see if she's got any better. But the tickets cost €400 and while Daddy is comfortable, he's not made of money. Four hundred was outrageous although they were in the front row; Xavier would not like to sit anywhere else. Still they were expensive, Daniel O'Dolan tickets cost €10 and I thought that was dear enough. You'd think Madonna would cop herself on, charging that much for tickets, still I suppose she needs it to keep up her appearance and she's buying a lot of orphanages in Africa too.

You really shouldn't begrudge your brother; he's on the dole, God love him and you have a grand job. If Gary was working ye'd be able to go grand places. Shur when he's on MTV you'll probably be hanging out with Madonna at the Ivy in London. All the same though I don't want you to feel left out so I'll get a ticket for you for Daniel O' Dolan the next time he's in Cork. I'll give you plenty of notice so you can book your flight.

Now I know you'll be all excited about your visitors but don't forget to phone Mammy immediately.

Love Mammy.

To: Kay@hotmail.com
Cc: Deirdre@aol.com ; Pearse@hotmail.com
From: Mammy@ eirecom
February 12th

Dear Dr Solomon
At last, a reply from you. I was just about to ring
your brothers to get Interpol to check if you were
still alive. How was I to know your computer's
memory could take no more. No more what
exactly? Perhaps you should buy a better system,
after all you are married to a plastic surgeon and
should have the best of everything including
appearance. Still it's all sorted out now so we can
get back to normal.

Daniel O' Dolan's mammy was not at the
concert either this time. He was his usual
entertaining self and his is still a fine man at 80.
It's a mystery why he never got married. I
suppose he was too devoted to his mother.
Xavier was up on the stage dancing with him all
night, it was a scream. Then believe it or believe it
or believe it not he took Xavier out for a meal
afterwards, we were invited too but I had to go
home to switch on Xavier's electric blanket
because it was very cold. Elvis Presley had
nothing on Daniel O 'Dolan. I know as I have seen
Elvis perform many times, on the tele. Daddy
used to think that he looked like Elvis, he did
alright but only during the week Elvis died. Ah

now, Daddy was a very good-looking man in his time; at least that's what his Mammy said anyway.

I was shocked by your attitude towards me buying Paul condoms for his Xmas stocking. Especially with you being a doctor. I am a modern mother you know. And I don't think the Catholic Church would see condoms as a form of contraception. In any case I had to do something as the withdrawal method is clearly not working. I am going to suggest to them now that she has her tubes tied after this one. Poor Paul will be exhausted bringing up 5 children and they're not the best behaved. In fact I think they are all hyperactive but that's the foxy hair you see. All people with foxy hair are hyperactive, that's why they always have big red faces, they are worn out from all the hyperactivity.
Love Mammy

To: Pearse@hotmail.com
Cc: Deirdre@aol.com ; Kay@hotmail.com;
From: Mammy@ eirecom.ie
February 13th

Dear All

I hate to be the one to tell ye but it's bad news here. Daddy has a broken ankle. It's his own fault; the lads and I told him to carry out the cases one at a time but no, he insisted on carrying four at a time. It was an accident waiting to happen. He said the doctor at the hospital said he should have called an ambulance immediately. Well that's all very well but would the doctor have taken the lads to the airport? I don't think so. In any case I've seen programmes on Bravo where Snowboarders carry on doing stunts with broken legs and arms and everything. And look at them women in Africa they have a baby and are back in their high heels and working in the office half an hour later. A broken ankle is nothing. I had a broken small toe once and I still managed to go dancing on the Saturday night.

The first thing I did was to ring Daddy's job and tell them that he would not be able to start and they said that was ok they would keep the job open for him. What kind of a place is that at all putting pressure on a sick man to come to work?

Now don't any of you be rushing home to look after Daddy. Timmy is off work till his hair grows back, the nuns said he was scaring the children down in the school. I suggested that he shave his head like all them balding men do but he said no he would rather let it grow and cut the other side up to match it then. I tried a comb-over but the scorched bits were still poking through.

So Timmy is moving in to look after Daddy for a few weeks. I couldn't be carrying him around, not with my brittle bone condition and my other problems. Of course Timmy can take me to where I need to go also which is just as well as I'm starting my psychology course on Monday week.

I'm all ready for the course now. They gave us a list of 30 books for suggested reading. Well you know me, I like to do everything correctly so I ordered all the books from Easons. When I went in to collect them I nearly died, €867.98. I had no idea that course books cost so much, but I have them now anyway. I bought a lovely gold pen too and a laptop. The laptop will be handy if I need to take work on holidays with me for urgent assessments.

Daddy and I were planning to go for a meal tonight, but he can't go now cause of his ankle. Timmy said he'll come with me. I had to refuse due to the state of his hair. Mr's D is coming instead. Daddy is paying.

Oh by the way don't be disappointed now if I can't email as regularly as normal. I have to prioritise my workload.
Love Mammy

To: Deirdre@aol.com
Cc: Pearse@hotmail.com ; Kay@hotmail.com;
From: Mammy@ eirecom.ie
February 14th

Dear Deirdre

Daddy is grand. He's lying around with his foot up. I tripped over him this morning and instead of asking me if I was alright he was screaming saying I'd knocked his foot down and would I look where I was going. He's very grumpy. Then he was cross again later because I gave Mrs D his painkillers as she had an awful hangover from last night. As you know I don't drink at all and Mrs D ordered non-alcoholic wine. Well I'd drank 17 glasses before she confessed that it wasn't non-alcoholic at all. We were screaming laughing after that. I'm grand anyway today just a bit of a headache from Daddy's bad temperedness.

So how are the lads? I bet you don't want them to come home tomorrow now. Well love all good things come to an end, and your loss is my gain, as far as Xavier is concerned, not Jeremy. I hardly know Jeremy. I hope you are making them a nice Sunday roast today. Xavier prefers beef. How did they get on at Madonna? I'd say now it's lucky that she didn't spot Xavier in the audience, she would have snapped him up. Although she is old enough to be his mother, still that never stopped her before.

Timmy will pick them up from the airport in the morning. He will be wearing a baseball cap. Not so that they can recognise him, Xavier knows who he is, but so that he can hide his hair.

I bought a lovely satin bed set for Xavier's bed as a little welcome home surprise. Also a tiny video-cam as the one he has is a bit big and therefore very heavy for him to be carrying. Daddy can take the old one to Italy if they go at all. They are humming and hawing about it now.

What are ye doing today?   I know you will be busy cooking and I suppose the lads will be down the pub for a lunchtime drink. It would be nice if the lads went out for a drink tonight with Gary as you will be busy washing and ironing Xavier's clothes for coming home tomorrow. Don't worry about packing till the morning. I find packing on the day of travel lessens wrinkles and creases. You will have plenty of time in the morning as the flights not till 6.30.

By the way if there is any change from Xavier's housekeeping €20 don't worry about sending it back. Keep it and buy yourself something with it unless he needs it for a cup of tea at the airport.
 Love Mammy

To: Pearse@hotmail.com
Cc: Deirdre@aol.com ; Kay@hotmail.com;
From: Mammy@ eirecom.ie
February 23rd

Dear Pearse

Thanks for your email, although it was a little offhand I felt, I am very sensitive to that sort of thing. How was I to know that the Chinese girl was a lawyer? In any case I don't think I said anything amiss. I was only trying to help with what I thought was a poor immigrant girl. I suppose the designer clothes should have given me a clue. Although in my defence, I do know for a fact that the best designer fakes come from China. My friend's hubby used to get us Louis V bags for a pound each during 2000 when he was doing business in China.

It's not my fault that you left my email open on your computer and it's hardly decent of her to read it. You know what they say about snoopers. Has she no sense of humour at all anyway, it was an honest mistake. I'm not sure if she could be a lawyer here now though, I think she might have to speak Irish. Anyone can be a lawyer in the Australia, but it's very different here. What was she doing round your place at that time in the morning anyway? Does she bring you breakfast on her way to work.

Daddy is grand, still in the plaster and still complaining. He has Timmy nearly driven mad.

I know this because Timmy snapped at Xavier on the phone earlier. Poor Xavier was on a lads' night out down town and somehow or another he got dropped off at a place miles out the country and he had no money to get a taxi. He rang Timmy's mobile at around 5am to come and get him. Now the funny thing was that Xavier was a bit tipsy and could not say where he was exactly. Well, Timmy let out a string of foul language and abuse, the likes of which I have never heard, then he told Xavier to feck off and went back to bed. All the commotion woke me up. Luckily I am a quick thinker and I immediately rang Paul. I asked him to utilise all the Garda forces in the area to find Xavier. You know they could use satellite technology to pinpoint the exact location of Xavier's mobile. I saw that on CSI. Paul said himself and the wife was had just got all the hyperactive foxy children to sleep and now, because of the phone ringing, they were all awake including the dog. He went on saying that Xavier is 32 years of age, older than himself and he would need to cop himself on and hung the phone up. Well, it's hardly my fault that he has all them children and a dog.

In the end I had to get Daddy up, I wanted him to ring his old Army buddy to see if the army could find Xavier but he said no. He went upstairs and got Timmy up and the two of them went out and got Xavier and they were all home by 7. I said to

Daddy if Timmy had just gone to get Xavier in the first place we could have avoided all that commotion. I said to Timmy to expect a few cross words from Paul as his refusal to deal with the situation had woken up the whole family.

Timmy said he might have to move home sooner than expected as his Mammy didn't sound too well on the phone last night. I said 'did she say she was sick'? He said 'no she wouldn't, as she would not want to be a burden'. I hope she's ok though as it will be a lot for Timmy having to look after his Mammy and your Daddy.
Love Mammy

To: Deirdre@aol.com
Cc: Pearse@hotmail.com ; Kay@hotmail.com;
From: Mammy@ eirecom.ie
March 1st

Dear Deirdre

In the first place I have not been avoiding you at all. Why would I. As I told you I hardly knew Jeremy and neither did Xavier. Xavier said he only met him at some club in town a couple of weeks ago. Therefore, for you to infer that I was avoiding you because Jeremy allegedly stole Gary's brand new iPod is total nonsense. It's nothing to do with me. Is Gary sure that he lent it to Jeremy?

Why would he lend a brand new iPod to a complete stranger? Shur for all we know that Jeremy could be an awful robber. In any case Gary could have lost that iPod anywhere he's an awful eejit when he's drunk and not too clever when he is sober either. The person who is really wronged here is poor Xavier. He was only helping Jeremy out taking him to London as apparently Jeremy had just broke up from his partner. Whether that was a business partner or wife I'm not sure. I don't pry. Now poor Xavier feels that Gary is hinting it's his fault that the iPod went missing. As Xavier said he has every iPod and music player ever made and he was even thinking of sending one of the cheaper ones over to Gary as a replacement. I don't think he will now after your email. Perhaps yourself and Gary will take a lesson from this and be more careful of the people you let stay in your home and also who you loan your belongings to.

Secondly, you could not have heard me shout 'if that's Deirdre tell her I'm out'. I was upstairs when the phone rang. Daddy just got mixed up and thought I had already gone out. I hadn't, but I was on my way out to the Psychology Class.

Psychology Class ha! There was false advertising if I ever saw it. A disaster from start to finish, someone should sue. It started off badly. Timmy was very slow carrying my books into the classroom and the teacher was standing there waiting to start. Timmy won't rush himself at all unless it's to get to the pub. Then the one who was teaching, Dr Higgins (although not a day's medical training behind her I'd say) said that as space was limited she would rather that I only bring the necessary writing paper and pen as she would give 'copies' of all relevant materials. Copies, if you don't mind, that course cost €350. I'd say she was jealous of all my books. Anyway she was waiting to introduce us to her colleague who would also be teaching us. If you saw him, he was a big hippy fella, I'd say his hair hadn't seen a brush since the 60's. 'Dr' Higgins was gazing up at him saying he had this qualification and that qualification. I put up my hand and asked if any of them had medical backgrounds, they said

39

no. I said I did have some medical training. As you know I have read all Kay's medical books so there's not much I don't know about medicine. The hippy said 'we can discuss that later during the break'. I thought to myself 'we will in my eye, discuss it later'. I knew very well what he wanted to discuss, believe you me. It's an awful problem but everywhere I go the men take a fancy to me, even if I say so myself I am very attractive with a lovely figure. If I had that big pink diamond ring it might put them off, but probably not.

Anyway, you could see that she was incensed by him taking a liking to me but she started the class. What a load of bloody rubbish. She was talking about Freud, who we all know needed a psychiatrist himself, the stuff he came out with should have been banned years ago. All he had on his mind was S E X. I asked her when we were going to get on to the criminals but she said we have to at least get the basis of the differing schools of thought before we can even look at the human mind. I said when will I be able to do profiling for police forces around the world and she said that would it would take years of studying before that could happen. Well now D, the course is only 3 months long so it seemed to me that there was no chance of my being a freelance profiler for the FBI as soon as the course finished. I told her that the course was obviously well below my level and I wanted my money back there and then. She said I would have to discuss that with the college administration people. She said I had obviously not read the course description properly. I said I had, and that she had obviously not written it properly implying that we would all be working for the FBI before the year was out. She asked me to leave as other people there wanted to learn. I said to them 'you'll learn nothing here lads' and off I went. I am going to get my money back tomorrow and Eason's can have their books back too although I have written my name in all of them.

I have decided to take Salsa lessons next week. I asked Daddy if he wanted to join but he said no, his ankle would not allow it.

Love Mammy

To: Kay@hotmail.com
Cc: Deirdre@aol.com ; Pearse@hotmail.com
From: Mammy@ eirecom.ie
March 8th

Dear Dr

I have decided to email you now only when you email me although I will still cc you on important matters. I wouldn't want to be a burden to you or want you to waste your valuable time reading news of your home and family.

I don't feel that I should apologise for emailing everyone on the hospital's email address as it was your lack of contact which forced my hand. Imagine the shame of a poor mother having to send a 'missing' poster of her daughter to 800 people just to make sure she was still alive. I really don't feel that it is my problem that the attached files were so big that they crashed the server. How is that my fault, surely a hospital should have a better network than that. Anyway, I don't know anything about computers as I have spent my whole life devoted to Daddy and my family.

Daddy is still in plaster and still taking advantage of the situation. I am worn out from him. Timmy is still here. He thought he might have to go home because his Mammy did not sound well but she was only drunk. Since Timmy has been here looking after Daddy, his mammy has started going out to a singles club and she has met a lovely fella. They are out on the town every night of the week and Mary-Anne has bought all new clothes from Penny's. As you know Timmy didn't like her going out at all as he likes a big fry-up when he gets home from the pub but her new fella is younger than Timmy and said that she deserves to be treated like a princess. He is from Russia and has bags of money so they can spend what they like on the craic. I said to Mary-Anne, 'it's lucky he's not Polish'. Timmy does not like Polish men because he was out one night with Daddy and had bought a sandwich. When Timmy went to the toilet Daddy eat the sandwich but he told Timmy a Polish fella eat it. There was nearly murder committed and since then Timmy is wary of Polish men. He did have a Polish girlfriend for a couple of weeks but she could not understand a word he was saying and she spoke perfect English.   The Russian has told Mary-Anne if Timmy gave her any problems he could arrange for Timmy to be 'spoken to'. I suppose he means by the priest. Not that Timmy would care about what the Pope said never mind a priest. They are gone away for the week now to Killarney for the festival (Mary-Anne and the Russian, not Timmy and the Pope). I'm sure they would have separate rooms.

I went to the Salsa class last night. The instructor was a Cuban man called Hosea. He had on the tightest trousers you ever saw.

Well that I ever saw anyway, I suppose you get loads of fellas wearing tight trousers in NY. He also had a slouch hat, an orange and white neckerchief and high-heeled boots. For some reason he had a plastic knife tucked into his belt.

He said he would have to divide us into sets depending on ability. He said the Beginners could go there, the Intermediates there and the Experienced there. I was the only one in the experienced group. As you know I watch all the dance programmes and know every dance there is to know. And as you know I am very light on my feet. I was delighted when he said as I was the most experienced dancer there I could partner him to give a demonstration. He asked what my favourite dance was and I said 'the Argentine Tango'. He said 'well then that is the dance we shall do, the mating dance, music maestro' and he ran over and turned on the cassette.

Well girl, I don't know what happened, somehow or another he got his legs tangled in mine, I think he didn't know the steps, and so it ended up with him on the floor screaming 'call an ambulance, I am in agony' (them Spanish types are very dramatic). I was hurt too although not physically, I had broken the heel of my new dancing shoes which cost €70 and that's only for one, the pair cost €140.

When the ambulance came it turned out that he had broken his right ankle and three toes on his left foot. He was saying to the ambulance men 'oh how will I pay my rent, this is my only income, oh sweet Jesus help me'. I asked him if he had any insurance so I can sue him, well he let out a stream of language that you wouldn't hear from a sailor. As they were putting him in the ambulance I asked could he give me my money back as the lessons were obviously cancelled. He said that I would get my money back when Hell freezes over. I was so upset that I had to phone Timmy to come and get me and I had to have 12 glasses of medicinal brandy to calm my nerves.

I am emailing Pearse to ask the Chinese lawyer about what my rights are.

Love Mammy

To: Deirdre@aol.com
Cc: Pearse@hotmail.com ; Kay@hotmail.com;
From: Mammy@ eirecom.ie

March 14th

Dear Deirdre

It was lovely talking to you on the phone last night. In fact it was nice that you were at home for once.

I have recovered now from the trauma of the Salsa class and am starting a course in Carpentry next week at the Technical College.

I know you don't like to upset me by asking about my health but ask away girl, shur I don't mind at all.

I have not been able to go back to the doctor's since January as Dr Nolan has been off. I ring every day to check if he's back and great news, he is definitely back next week. It's not before time as I am not well. I think that the brittle bone is worse and my feet have been killing me for the last week. I will let you know anyway how I get on. I was on the verge of getting a new Doctor but I'm used to Dr Nolan and I would not want to offend him by seeing anyone else.

Daddy is grand although he says he's tired. What he's tired from I don't know, all he does is sit around all day with the leg up. He doesn't feel tired at all when it's time to go to the pub.

Auntie Mary-Anne is madly in love with the Russian. She said he is handsome. Mrs D and myself are going to meet him when they come back from Ibiza next weekend. He takes her all over the place. First Killarney and now Ibiza. Mary-Anne bought a box of glow-sticks to take to Ibiza. Timmy is not happy about the romance at all, although he hasn't met the Russian yet. I think Timmy should start thinking about settling down himself. He's 31 now and no oil painting. He's a bit like a fat Robbie Williams. He was engaged to Julie for 8 years but he said she was pressuring him to name the day so he gave her up. She's married now to a lovely butcher from Blackrock. Timmy still sees the six kids. I said to him the other night that himself and Xavier should go out looking for girlfriends but he was only laughing at me.

I'd say he might be a bit jealous of Xavier's good looks and designer wardrobe. In any case I don't think Xavier is ready to settle down yet. He is in Ibiza with Mary-Anne and the Russian, the Russian paid for his holiday, isn't that nice of him. I gave him Xavier a small bit of spending money as they have lovely leather things in Spain and Xavier wanted one of those leather suits worn by the Beckhams a while back.
Love Mammy

To: Deirdre@aol.com
Cc: Pearse@hotmail.com ; Kay@hotmail.com;
From: Mammy@ eirecom.ie
March 20th

Dear Deirdre

Well now it's been ages since I heard from you so I hope you are ok and eating well. Don't eat too much though as you would not want to get heavy. Stay as slim as you are.

I got to see Dr Nolan, at last, and he's sending me for a bone scan next week.

I asked him if he'd enjoyed his holiday in Venezuela and he said he did not want to come back to face, and I quote, 'the Hell that is my life here'. He said that he has certain patients that waste his time and resources (some people, like Daddy, go to the doctor if they sneeze) and that he wished he had bought a gun in Venezuela and either shot himself there and then or brought it home and shot the patients he was alluding to. I said to him that 'I think you would find that you would never be able to get a gun either out of Venezuela or into Ireland due to increased security because of the alleged increase in international terrorist attacks, so you would have been better off shooting yourself there and then'. He said he might have been better off had he got the gun, got caught with it at Caracas Airport and been arrested and put to prison in Venezuela.

Says I, to myself like, wake up now boy and smell the roses. If he was working down a mine all day he'd have something to complain about.

Still, though that's an awful way for a doctor to be talking. I suggested to him that he prescribe himself some strong anti-depressants (monoamine oxidase inhibitors in my opinion are best) or go into town and buy a bag of magic mushrooms, for medicinal purposes obviously. Then I asked him for some sleeping-pills to slip into Daddy's cocoa and he said he might as well and save himself the trouble. I don't know what he was talking about, but I'm telling you this; it's a sad day for the medical profession when a patient has to give the doctor advice and I still had to pay him €30. I turned around to say something as I was leaving and I could have sworn he was drinking from a whiskey bottle.

I told Timmy all about it when we got out and Timmy said did I need a brandy to calm my nerves and I said no as I don't drink at all only for medicinal purposes in times of great stress.

Timmy's hair is growing in a bit now but he still looks like an awful eejit. I was ashamed of my life walking down to the car-park with him because we met Julie and she could not stop laughing. Then when she was gone Timmy started crying saying he wished now he'd married her and he wouldn't be in the mess he's in. But he would have been; Gary would still have dragged him out to the pub on Xmas eve.

Xavier will be home from Ibiza later on and Mr's D and myself are going to meet the Russian tomorrow night. I asked Timmy if he wanted to come and he said he would rather eat his own heart than see his mammy with a toy-boy (I hope to God that's not a bit of the Oedipus complex). I said 'please yourself so'. Then Timmy said did I think the Russian would be buying free drinks all night and I said 'probably' and he said he might come so.

The school is refusing to pay his sick pay because the burnt hair is not an illness and also it was self-inflicted. I don't know who's looking after the convent now that he's off. I said to him 'Timmy every cloud has a silver lining because if you were not off Daddy would have no-one to look after him'. I think that cheered him up a bit.
Love Mammy

To: Kay@hotmail.com
Cc: Deirdre@aol.com ; Pearse@hotmail.com
From: Mammy@ eirecom.ie
March 25th

Dear Kay,
I don't want you to be upset but I am giving up
addressing you as Dr. After 3 years I'm finding it
doesn't amuse me anymore.

It was very nice to hear from you although it's a
pity that it's little and not often. I am delighted that
Jerry has been appointed to the hospital Board of
Directors. I hope it won't make him any bigger-
headed than he already is, ha-ha.

It's lovely now that you've both been invited to
The Children's Health Fund Gala Dinner with a
performance by Jennifer Lopez at the NY Hilton. I
looked it up on the Internet and the tickets cost
$1000 each and tables between $10000 and
$100000. I'd expect Jennifer Lopez to come and
sing in my front room for that. Make sure now you
wear a nice frock and buy some diamante
jewellery. It's a pity you're not here as Argos have
a lovely range of diamante jewellery at very
reasonable prices. A little bit of exercise wouldn't
go amiss either as you looked a small bit hefty in
the latest photos. If it's cold wear your coat, but
not that blue one you had over here last year.

Now as you know Xavier absolutely loves
Jennifer Lopez so he was wondering if you could
get hold of another ticket for him. If not do you

think Jerry might be willing to let Xavier have his ticket as Jerry is not really a Gala kind of guy and Xavier is far better looking and a lot slimmer. Xavier will wear his new leather Gucci suit he got in Ibiza and don't worry, it's not old fashioned, it's the newest one. Let me know as soon as you can as I will have to make all the travel arrangements for Xavier.

I went for the bone scan this morning and your one said she would contact Dr Nolan with the results. I wanted her to tell me there and then and prescribe me something to begin my treatment immediately but she couldn't as she is only a Radiographer. I said 'I bet you're sorry now that you did not go to Medical School'. She said she did but I don't think so. Why would she be a Radiographer if she did?

Daddy gets the plaster removed next week and he says he will have a big surprise for me, I bet it's that lovely ring to say thanks for the sacrifices I made while looking after him. It will be no harm to have the house back to normal when Timmy goes home. Every night this week the two of them have been down at Danny Mac's bar and then they are singing downstairs till all hours. It's a wonder the neighbours don't call the guards. Although Mr Ahern came to complain the other night about all the noise and then Daddy insisted that he come in and join them and now he's going to the pub every

night too. Mrs A is raging as Mr was a teetotaller until he started hanging around with Daddy and Timmy. He took the Pledge when he was 18 and stuck with it till last Tuesday and he's 51 now. I said to Mrs A, 'it's no good complaining to me, shur I don't drink at all. I said to her why don't you try it yourself and see how you get on'? She said she's worried about her figure. I said, to myself, 'I wouldn't bother. It wouldn't really matter how slim you were as your face will still be the same'.
Love Mammy

To: Pearse@hotmail.com
Cc: Deirdre@aol.com ; Kay@hotmail.com;
From: Mammy@ eirecom.ie
April 2nd

Dear Pearse
Thanks for ringing last night. I am very sorry about not winning the Euro Millions but I only phoned your boss and told him that as an April fool's trick. I'm sorry to disappoint you and it's hardly my fault that you boss was 'not happy'. How was I to know he would be paged away from his mother's funeral. I didn't even know she was dead. Some people have no sense of humour. Pearse, I hate to say it like, but you seem to be losing your own sense of humour too boy.

Well, we all went to meet the Russian last week. Timmy came in the end although he would only order his drinks through Daddy and did not say a word to his mother or the Russian all night. The Russian is a very nice fella with blonde hair. He seems madly in love with Mary-Anne. Mary-Anne was like a teenager, all giggling and swinging her hair around. Her hair is not short and grey anymore, she had what she called a 'weave' done in Ibiza and it's all long blonde curls with a big beehive on top. She had on a ton of makeup but I suppose she wants to look good as the Russian is only 21. She had on a cropped top and shorts but really, I don't think it was very flattering as she is a size 18. She had on gorgeous high-heeled glass platform shoes although Xavier said they were generally known as stripper shoes. In any case she kept twisting her ankle in them once she'd had a few drinks. I was drinking 'Bloody Mary's' all night. I thought they were with tomato juice and some hot sauce added in but by the time I found out they had vodka in them I had already finished throwing up in the toilet. Apparently, I should have ordered Virgin Marys. Xavier and the Russian got on like a house on fire and they were laughing and joking all night.

The next day Timmy took Daddy to get the plaster off his leg and when they came back from the hospital I asked Timmy what time he was going home to his mother. Daddy has a walking stick so Timmy said he was going to stay until Daddy is back to normal. I was on the verge of telling him to go home but Daddy said he can't drive for another few weeks so I let him stay. I did not get the diamond ring. The big surprise was that he could walk with a walking stick and not crutches. I'm sure some people would say that that is better than a diamond ring but I would not be one of them.

Did Marie tell you her news. She has a boyfriend. Jaysus, if you saw him. He has a face only his mother could love. He dresses like herself in all that black and his make-up is applied with a trowel by the looks of it. His name is Chris and I asked him if he wanted me to show him how to apply make-up properly but he said no thanks. Apparently they have known each other for a few months and have been living together for 3 weeks. I didn't even know she had moved out I thought she was either in her bedroom or out. It's all Daddy's fault, I tell you I'm losing my mind looking after him. Daddy, however, knew all about it and said it's fine for them to live together as long as it does not interfere with her studies. I never thought now that she'd get a boyfriend but life is full of little surprises. She is still as contrary as ever. Now that she's moved out she wants her bedroom re-decorated and rented out to some friends she's got coming over from the US for three months in the summer. She will use the rent to buy eyeliner and fishnet tights. I would not allow that at all, what would I know about Americans.

As I had not heard from Dr Nolan regarding my bone scan I rang the surgery to speak to him but the receptionist (the receptionist if you don't mind) told me that the results would take up to four weeks to come back and they would call me if the doctor needed to speak to me. I said to her 'why do I have to wait four weeks, all they have to do is put them in an envelope, put a stamp on and post them'. She said 'no, they have to be analyzed by the specialist at the lab'. I said 'I will ring every day to check if they are back', she said, in a very curt manner, that they would call me when the results are back. What could I do?

I am just on my way out now to meet Xavier as he needs a new mobile phone, he's had the other one a couple of months now but it is very out-of-date and there is a new one out that he wants. He is on 'pay-as-you-go' as Daddy refused to set up a direct debit with the bank. I get him €50 credit every Saturday.

I start carpentry class tomorrow, I'd say I'll be really good at that as I love Ty in Extreme Makeover Home Edition©.
Love Mammy

To: Deirdre@aol.com
Cc: Pearse@hotmail.com ; Kay@hotmail.com;
From: Mammy@ eirecom.ie
April 8th

Dear Deirdre

Thanks for your flowers for Mother's Day, which
came on the day before Mother's Day itself. It
would be really nice if florists delivered on the
actual day, they charge enough. Pearse and Kay
actually phoned me on the day so I thanked them
in person then. Your card came a few days late
and funnily enough Kay's came all the way from
America and Pearse's came all the way from
Australia and they were both on time.

What a surprise Mrs D had on Mother's Day.
She was doing her morning ablutions when there
was a loud knock at the door. She opened the
door and on the mat was a huge card and a
beautifully wrapped box, inside the card was €200
and a 1 week gift certificate for the Presidential
Suite at Hayfield Manor, which is a superior Health
Spa. Now as if that was not enough, in the
present box was a platinum chain as thick as the
Lord Mayor's chain with a diamond the size of a
conker on it. Well she said she was overcome.
How does Tina manage to think of these things
and still manage to look her best at all times. Of
course Tina is tall, it's a pity that none of my girls
are tall really, height is very important for looking

good. Mrs D is so lucky but to be honest she said she would never wear the chain as she would feel like a homie.

Well, Mrs D said the overall effect of Tina's plan was only spoilt by Mr D. He had had the card and present since Friday and he was supposed to put them outside and knock on the door and then run upstairs. Unfortunately, he locked himself out and had to climb over the fence into the back garden. He got the collar of his shirt stuck on the point of the fence and nearly choked to death. It was lucky the man next door was out doing the garden as he heard Mr D gurgling and got him down just in time. Mrs D said he ruins everything, but as I said 'he's a man'.

Xavier bought me a lovely garden ornament, and Mrs Lynch next door said 'coincidentally the very same ornament was stolen from her front garden during the night'. I said 'isn't that strange now'. Xavier made me a lovely card from the cornflake box, he is very artistic. Xavier says making a card takes a lot more thought than buying one in a shop. Although Xavier went for the minimalist message and just wrote 'Happy Mammy's Day Mammy' in pencil. He is very conscious of re-cycling and does not want to be using up too many pencils as trees have to be cut down to make pencils.

Well Marie has broken up with the ugly fella and moved back in, he was not that ugly really I suppose. She said that he wanted her to go to the laundrette with him to wash his clothes. She brought her own washing home for Timmy to do so, as she said, why would she want to watch his washing going round and round. Also she said no-one had done any washing-up in the 3 weeks they were there and they had no clean glasses to drink their cider from. She's better off at home anyway. Daddy was not a bit happy about paying her share of the rent. She now wants Daddy to give her the money he would have spent on her rent so he's no better off.

Carpentry class was not good at all. I had bought all my own tools, I ordered them off the internet from Rinaldi in Italy, the best tools available and used by professionals apparently. So off I went with Timmy and as usual we were late setting off because it took Timmy so long to load the tools in the car and Daddy could only carry the light things, he needs to sort himself out really if he is to be of any use.

We weren't too late getting to the college but Timmy took ages to bring my tools in and then the man said he would have to take them all back out as the tools were already supplied in the workshop. Timmy was stomping in and out and in the end the man and some of the other students gave him a hand. The man said that this was level 3 Carpentry and Joinery. I don't know what joinery is though and probably never will now as the man said that making a few Airfix plane kits did not qualify me to be at Level 3 and that it would not matter if I had watched every DIY programme in the world it wouldn't make any difference. If I wanted to do Carpentry and Joinery I would have to start at the 'Introduction to Woodwork'. I wouldn't dream of doing an Introduction to anything, I am well past Introduction level in everything. I had made a bookshelf from MFI; why would I want to go back to making a feckin mug rack. Mug racks are not even in fashion these days.

I'm a bit fed up to tell the truth because my plans of building on a conservatory myself won't come to fruition. I asked Daddy if we can hire a company to build one and he said the money I spent on the books, tools, shoes and classes would have paid for a new house to be built never mind a conservatory. He does exaggerate at times. I said to him that I was too disappointed to organise sending the tools back so himself and Timmy would have to do it after all we can't just leave them lying around the place.

I am thinking of doing a Reggae course in a couple of weeks.
Love Mammy

To: Pearse@hotmail.com
Cc: Deirdre@aol.com ; Kay@hotmail.com;
From: Mammy@ eirecom.ie
April 16th

Dear Pearse,
I'm delighted now that everything is back to normal
at work.   I would imagine it is difficult to work
under an atmosphere.   I was sorry to hear that the
Chinese girl broke it off with you. I don't think now
my phoning her at the office to ask about suing the
Salsa man had anything to do with it.   I hope it
didn't like as that is her job after all. I *had* to
reverse the charges as it's very expensive to
phone Australia and Daddy retired very young. As
Mrs D said they didn't have to accept the calls if
they didn't want to.   Oh and her saying that I sent
her hundreds of emails is a bit of an exaggeration.
In any case the advice she would have given me
would have been useless as that's Australian law
and not like real law at all.   Really now though
don't take it so hard, you would be much better off
with a nice Irish girl. Just make sure she doesn't
have ginger hair. Although I suppose nobody in
Australia has ginger hair as they would die in the
sun.

    Great news for you now, Xavier and his little
friend are applying for visas to Australia and they
will be coming to stay with you for 18 months.
Xavier is taking a few gap years before he starts

university. I'm not sure yet which uni he will go to but I pray that it's UCC so he can come home every day. I said to Daddy that I was worried he might choose to go to Harvard or Yale but Daddy said I had no need to worry about that at all. Daddy can be nice when he wants to.

Now isn't it lucky I made you have that sofa-bed shipped over, I know you said it cost you a fortune but you'll have the use of it now, when the lads get there. I did say to Xavier that you had only the one bedroom, but he said himself and Dec don't mind sharing at all. Of course you sleeping on the sofa-bed in the living/dining room/kitchen will be very handy as you won't have to wake the lads when you are going out to work in the morning. And now that the Chinese girl has found herself a better prospect you will be glad of the company. You'll have a great laugh with the 3 of ye going out on the lash. Australian mothers lock up your daughters, the boys are back in town!!

I'll wait a while now before I give you all the instructions regarding Xavier's dietary requirements, laundry requirements etc. In fact, what I will do nearer the time is email you each list separately and then you can print them out and have them laminated. Then you can put them on the wall so you don't get mixed up and there are no mishaps. Don't forget to buy blue tack or whatever they call it down under.

If I'm to be perfectly honest now Pearse I really don't want Xavier to go away for that long at all. Mrs D doesn't want him to go either as she loves our nights out, but his new little friend Dec really feels that they should broaden their horizons. Why they can't go on the boat to the Isle of Man for a weekend is beyond me. All groups of lads go over there for the craic. Timmy has been I don't know how many times.

Well that brazen trollop of a receptionist rang from Dr Nolan's and said that my bone scan had come back clear. I said did that mean my bones were so far gone they could see through them a little sarcasm never goes amiss with Doctors' receptionists. She said no, it meant that my bones were normal for a woman my age. I said' I need to see Dr Nolan immediately, obviously someone, probably yourself has made a mistake'. She said 'Dr Nolan is away in the Isle of Man'. I said 'can I have his new mobile number as the one I have does not work anymore', she said 'no she was not at liberty to give out that information'. I said 'when will he be back' and she said 'next week' so I am making another appointment with Dr Nolan to ask for an MRI scan. I'd say now that would show anything up. I told the receptionist that I was not at all impressed with her attitude and I would be thinking long and hard about reporting her to the Department of Health and Children. I told you that radiographer didn't have a clue what she was doing. Now I have to go through it all again.

Well son, take care of yourself now and make sure you dry your washing properly as you'd get an awful cold from damp clothes. Xavier said to ask you if you know Kylie Minouge and if you do can you ask her to write to him. He said do <u>not</u> give her his number just his address, he wouldn't want anyone ringing him up all the time.

Love Mammy

To: Kay@hotmail.com
Cc: Deirdre@aol.com ; Pearse@hotmail.com
From: Mammy@ eirecom.ie
April 20th

Dear Kay

Well I'm sure we are all delighted that you had a chat with Jennifer Lopez. Mrs D's girl Tina has a maid call Jenny Lopez. Do you have any maid at all? I don't remember you saying that you do and I am sure you would have said. But then Tina's hubby is something on Wall Street and money is no object. The photos are lovely, yourself and Jerry look like film stars.

Poor Xavier was bereft when you rang and said that Jerry wanted to go to the Gala himself, and there were no more tickets left. To cheer him up I had to go online and get him VIP tickets for Cher in Las Vegas when he goes over on his holidays next week. He said 'thanks Mammy' but God love him, he could not raise a smile, he does love Jenny. What would Jerry know about J Lo anyway, as Xavier said 'Jerry never came from the block'.

Are you and Jerry able to go to Malibu for a few days to see Xavier? He will be there from April 23rd to May 1st. Then he will be moving on to Vegas. He will be staying at the Crescent Hotel - an elegant LA boutique hotel which combines refined American gloss with laid-back California sunshine. Minimal-chic interiors by design impresario Dodd Mitchell nestle modestly behind a stucco facade, and the restaurant is a star attraction – literally. It's only $600 a night each so yourself and Jerry should have no problems staying there, especially with friends like Jennifer Lopez.

It would be nice if you and Jerry would take Xavier out for a shopping trip on Rodeo Drive. He is on the dole after all. It might help him to move on after the Jennifer Lopez affair.

Daddy is getting around much better now and will soon be back in the driving seat, it won't be any harm for Timmy to go home. I'm fed up of him moping around the place. He has been feeling down since that day when we met Julie, now she was looking lovely but as I said to him, 'Timmy you were the one that ended it, Julie has moved on to better prospects, so cop yourself on now and get your head shaved and get back to work'. Tough love works you know. I told him 'you will never get anyone as good as Julie again, you're not getting any younger, any richer, any slimmer or any more attractive so you may very well have to accept that you might spend the rest of your life alone. Even your Mammy has someone now so she won't have much time for keeping you company'. I think that might help him to get himself sorted out. Sometimes the cold, harsh truth is the best catalyst.

Paul was down today all flustered about Nora's, work partner that drives around in the squad car with her. Paul said 'now Mammy as you know I am not racist', I said 'I know that love, you would never be allowed in the Gardai if you were racist', 'but' he says, 'I don't like that African fella that Nora has for a partner, when I got home this morning he was fast asleep in our bed. Now Nora wasn't there as she was on duty, but I'm not happy that she gave him a key, I had to go and sleep in the twin's room on the floor'. I was taken aback really, I had no idea at all that Nora had given her partner a key, I didn't even know she had a new partner.

Giving him a key though, is she mad, the house will be full of Africans before she knows it. They are very family orientated and like to live together, still at least she would have lots of babysitters and Paul could have some time to play sports and go to the pub with the lads. I told Paul I would have a word with her. He said 'thanks mammy'.

I asked Daddy to drive me down to the station to see Nora but he said he cannot due to his ankle, so I phoned Timmy who was in town putting an ad in the 'Lonely Hearts/Desperate Singles' column in the Echo to come and take me.

When I got to the station I asked for Nora and out she comes all smiles. I was in no mood for her smiling, in any case once she saw Timmy she was not smiling anymore she feels that Timmy is too familiar with the station and the lads on the desk there. I asked her what on earth the African garda was doing asleep in Paul's bed. She gave me the height of cheek. She said 'in the first place, Cecil is an Afro-American who had never been to Africa in his life. In the second place Cecil is a high-level detective from San Francisco who was over here giving advice on policing drug smugglers. In the third place Cecil had been assigned as my partner six months ago and I thought it would be a nice gesture between the Irish and American peoples to offer him a family home to stay in for the last part of his visit. Finally the only reason he was in my bed was because one of the twins had had an accident in the night'. She said too that she would have a few words to say to Paul for involving his family in her business. I said to her 'do too girl, he shouldn't be upsetting you now when you are pregnant'.

Paul, indeed all of you, are lucky that I am the kind of mother that has devoted her life to Daddy and yourselves and am not the kind of mother to get involved with her children's' business unless I feel that I must.

I have to say now that I am not feeling myself at all. It's nothing to do with my heads or my bones, I don't know what it is.

I am very tired and feeling sick. I dread to think
what could be wrong, it could be something
terrible. Say a prayer for me.
Love Mammy

To: Deirdre@aol.com
Cc: Pearse@hotmail.com ;
From: Mammy@ eirecom.ie
April 20th

Dear Deirdre

Well girl, did you ever see the like of the email
from Kay. She was delighted that she had a chat
with Jennifer Lopez. I mean who cares? Not me,
that's for sure. I don't like name droppers at all.
Kay never even mentioned the night that Xavier
went out for a meal with Daniel O' Dolan, but you
can bet your bottom dollar that she told Jennifer
Lopez about it

What about the photos, Daddy said they looked
like film stars, I said 'that would depend on which
film star you mean'. I thought they both looked a
bit heavy, Jerry is a plastic surgeon, he should be
able to make Kay as slim as she likes, yet he
doesn't seem to have done any work at all to her.

I am thinking of going over to NY to have some
work done myself. Not a great deal now, as I am
aging gracefully but you know a little nip here and
a little tuck there. I know what you're thinking,
won't that make me even more attractive to men,
but Deirdre we all have a cross to bear. I mean as
we have a plastic surgeon in the family, we may
as well make use of him, I might bring Mary-Anne
with me. She could do with a few stone suctioned
out and a face and breast lift. She needs to look
her best for the Russian after all. The only thing

though is that Jerry would have to guarantee that I would not be mugged by the 'Latin Kings'.

Mary-Anne and the Russian are in Galway this week at the festival. She is having a ball but she said she was having to take dozens of Pro-plus to stay awake till after 11 every night. I said perhaps she could try the new Ecstasy pill that they all talk about , it's supposed to be great for keeping you awake. She said she thought that might be illegal. I said I would ask Paul as he is a garda. But surely something with a lovely name like Ecstasy couldn't be illegal. Now heroin I can understand being illegal, and crack cocaine, but Ecstasy sounds grand. She said she has not said the Rosary for weeks.

I'm trying to bear up here but am heartbroken over Xavier going to Australia. I don't know what the house will be like without him and as well as that you know all them Australians are descended from English ex-cons and Xavier is a delicate little chap. If anything happened to him out there I would blame Pearse, if he wasn't there in the first place Xavier would not even think of going. God willing he might meet a lovely girl here and fall in love and then stay at home where he belongs.

How is Gary, did he get any job yet? Could he not get a little part-time job in McDonalds or somewhere? Tell him I said to give it a try anyway, there's no shame in failing.
Love Mammy

To: Kay@hotmail.com
Cc: Deirdre@aol.com ; Pearse@hotmail.com
From: Mammy@ eirecom.ie
April 22nd

Dear Kay

Well I am a bit bemused (to say the least) by your email saying you can't go to see Xavier. I mean how often is it that your brother goes to the States. Xavier himself said he didn't mind as he was linking up with some friends from the Internet. But as you know he is so innocent they could be anyone. If some American girl now gets her claws into him and he comes home married I will hold yourself and Jerry responsible. I sometimes get the feeling that you are getting too big for your boots Kay, but just remember if Jerry ran off and married Jennifer Lopez , the only people you would have to turn to are your family. After all you are not getting any younger.

Well enough of the unpleasantness now, as long as you know how I feel then that's fine. I have devoted my life to Daddy and my family and have never asked for anything in return as you well know. I understand that you both have to work but if Jerry is on the 'Board', a few days off should not be a problem, otherwise what use is being on the 'Board'.

I hope now that Xavier will be ok out there in L.A. You know that's the home turf of the Bloods and the Crypts and all sorts of gangsters. It's also where that Manson man was and I'm sure that fella Swarzenagger lives there as well, although I might be wrong. Just to be on the safe side, I have emailed the Los Angeles County Sherriff's Department and asked them to send a couple of officers to the airport to protect Xavier from the moment he lands. That is their job after all and I am sure that they would not like their Tourist Industry to be damaged by any bad publicity. The Sheriff's name is Sheriff Lee Baca. I told them Xavier would be wearing his Gucci leather suit and his D&G sunglasses and he has his hair in a pob with loads of blonde highlights. They'll be delighted when they see him and what a surprise it will be for Xavier to have a couple of friends.

I went to see Dr Nolan yesterday morning and to be honest with you he was quite strange, I hope he is not prescribing medication for himself. Anyway I said I wanted an MRI scan immediately and he said that there was a bit of a wait. I said to him, 'just put me to the top of the queue, I'm sure nobody would mind a sick mother of six getting a bit of priority treatment'. He said he would. I told him I was feeling strange, and he said 'would that be stranger than usual or a different strange to usual', I had no idea what he was talking about but I said 'a different strange'. Then I said to him 'you have an awful tic there in your left eye, you would need to do something about that as it makes you look a bit like a serial killer, and it could upset your patients, not myself now like as we are more like old friends'. He said 'thanks for bringing it up'. I said not to mention it. But to be honest with you I am thinking of reporting him to the Department of Health and Children because I am feeling a bit used as that's twice now that I have had to give him advice and pay him €30 each time for the honour, it's legalized robbery because you have to go to the doctor, it is not a leisure activity like and with me being delicate I probably have to go more than most so I am paying for Dr Nolan's jet-setting lifestyle. Hm.

I have to go now as Xavier is leaving for the airport soon.
Love Mammy

To: Deirdre@aol.com
Cc: Pearse@hotmail.com ; Kay@hotmail.com;
From: Mammy@ eirecom.ie
April 30th

Dear Deirdre

I am very lonely without Xavier but he will be home in a few days now so everything will be back to normal then. I have put Easter on hold until he gets back as he loves finding the Easter Eggs that I hide for all the kids in the garden. In fact last year Paul's children were all crying saying that Xavier took their eggs. Shur they were not their eggs at all, I hid them for everyone. I thought it was very nice for all of them to be able to join in the hunt for the eggs as that is half the fun.

This year Paul and Nora had their own Easter and no-one was invited except the Afro-American high-ranking detective in the Chicago Police Force. Paul was on duty at the Easter Parade but was home for his dinner later. The dinner was Beef, Pork, Rabbit and Seafood with vegetables which included okro, black eyed peas, tomatoes, peaches, broccoli, watermelon, eggplant, sesame seed, sorghum, and collard green. Now did you ever hear the likes of that for an Easter dinner? Paul said it was gruesome but he had to eat it as Nora is not on the best of terms with him at the moment. I said to Paul he can come here for the traditional Irish Easter dinner when Xavier comes home. Nora will think he's at work. He said he would see if he could slip in that day alright.

Well the Reggae Course was not what I thought at all. It was in fact a disaster. I had bought a lovely home entertainment system and all Bob Marley's records and indeed many of the today's Reggae stars' records too, including but not limited to Sean Paul, Cham, Damien Marley, Elephant Man and Beenie Man. I wanted the whole range.

I was getting well into the rhythm and even watching all the dancehall moves on Base MTV. As you know I have always liked to keep on top of what music is popular so I can converse with anyone, young or old, and as I know all there is to know about all other genres of music I thought I would give Reggae a go. I bought a lovely striped beanie hat and wore it to the first class. I didn't take my records or my home entertainment system as I had learned from earlier experiences.

Well when I got to the class there was not one young Afro-Caribbean person there. In fact it was all middle-aged women and one oul fella. Then in walked the teacher. It was not a nice young Afro-Caribbean man with dreads, it was a big fat woman with wild orange hair wearing a kaftan. I knew as soon as I laid eyes on her we would not get on at all. I should have left there and then but I had paid my money, €120, and after the trouble I had trying to get my money back from the Salsa fella I thought I'd see what she had to say for herself. Well she says 'I am delighted to see you all here today (it was evening like), and welcome and I am sure you will be amazed and spiritually uplifted by the journey we are about to take together'. I was wondering then at that point whether or not she was going to give us drugs to smoke; as nice as Reggae is, it's hardly amazing and while it can get you to have a bit of a dance, I'm not sure about spiritually uplifting. I decided there and then that if drugs were part of the curriculum I would have to give it a go, as I felt sure that if she was going to be handing drugs out to us then they must be legal for teaching Reggae. I would, of course confirm that with Paul, but if she was going to give us some tonight I would take the chance without Paul's ok.

Anyway she says 'using Reggae you will learn simple methods and techniques to bring pain and stress relief to your life. Practice techniques to share this loving and healing energy with yourself, your loved ones, and with the community. Send this loving and healing energy to even those who are far away from you. Reggae works for those near to you and those who live across the world. Reggae brings us all close together. It's perfect for adults as well as children to learn and use. Great to use on your plants and your pets'.

I just raised my hand, very cool now like, and said 'in the name of the Good Lord what are you on about, Reggae is good music, no doubt about it, but you are off your game if you think that it heals and you can use it on your plants and pets, what is that all about'. Then I started laughing fully expecting the others to laugh too. Your one gave me a look; she said to me 'what on earth are you talking about'? I knew she didn't like me, probably jealousy as I was looking exceptionally well-groomed although I suppose she would have been jealous no matter what I was looking like.

She said 'there has obviously been some sort of misunderstanding, we are here to learn Reike, a system of Natural Healing using hand positions to send Universal Life Force Energy to areas in need of attention'. I said 'are you kidding me here now, people will pay good money to learn that stuff'. I looked around me and I did notice that the others were all weird looking alright. I said 'well you might be fooling this bunch but you are not fooling me for a minute, I mean what are doctors for?' I said 'I want my money back right now or I am not moving', she said 'you will have to sort that out with the admin people'. I said 'it was they who got me into this mess in the first place, by not telling me exactly what this course was. She said 'they would have sent you the literature about the course'. I told her I did not get any literature, I did get a letter alright but I didn't have time to read it. The letters are pages long, I threw it in the bin. I said 'I'm waiting for my money' she said, 'if you

don't leave now I will have security come and remove you, you are wasting the learning time of these people'. I said 'it's you who are wasting their time and if this Reiki is so great why don't you use it to cure your obesity'? Then I marched out with my head held high. The cheek of some people.
Love Mammy

To: Kay@hotmail.com
Cc: Deirdre@aol.com ; Pearse@hotmail.com
From: Mammy@ eirecom.ie
May 5th

Dear Kay

Xavier is home. He liked America and met lots of his friends from the net. Which was just as well really as his own family and the American law would have left him to the perils of LA. He brought me home a lovely postcard of Rodeo Drive, he is very thoughtful as you know. Unlike some I could mention. Well I was horrified when he told me there were no policemen there to meet him. I am writing to the Head of the Homeland Security in America and asking him/her to launch an investigation into this matter. I specifically emailed and told the Sheriff all the details of Xavier's arrival so there are no excuses really. Would you ask Jennifer Lopez if she would write to him/her too as having a famous person writing might make things go a bit quicker. Tell her that I would be grateful if she could give this her full and immediate attention.

Well now Daddy is back to normal, well what passes as normal for him, the walking stick is gone, one of Paul's children set it on fire on the barbecue out in Paul's back garden, I told Timmy not to give him the lighter, but you may as well be talking to the wall. Paul's boys seem to be very interested in fires and matches and lighters. I expect they will be fire-fighters. Anyway rather than go and get another walking stick Daddy decided to do without. It's no harm really as he didn't look very attractive hobbling around with it. He looked like an old man and I was ashamed to be seen out with him.

Well now girl, as you know I am well known for my compassion and understanding nature and sometimes I wish I wasn't. People can take advantage of a nature like mine and make me feel like I am carrying the weight of the world on my shoulders. As well as that I have enough problems of my own with all of ye and Daddy and my poor health. Which reminds me no news about the MRI scan, I will get Daddy to phone Dr Nolan later. I have an appointment anyway at the end of the month as I have a bit of a personal problem which I don't want to discuss as no woman likes to talk about hair growing in strange and unusual places.

Well anyway back to my compassionate nature. I have been sworn to secrecy but Mrs. D is having marriage problems. Mr. D doesn't know. She got married very young, 16 and they are married 34 years now. She said that the first 33⅔ years were grand but after seeing Mary-Anne and the Russian she now feels that she wasted her youth. I said did she like Daniel O'Dolan and she said no he was old enough to be her father. Not that Daniel would bother with her like, she's no oil painting. Anyway she said that she is thinking now of going to the singles club with Mary-Anne and the Russian although I'm not sure if they still go there as technically they are not single now. I said to her that although I was very nearly a child bride myself, I have no experience of singles clubs and was not sure what went on there. I also said I have no experience of marriage problems. I said 'would you not be better off now devoting the rest of your life to your children and husband like I do, after all you are no spring chicken and you don't really have that long to go now, do you really want to be starting all over again'. She said 'yes'. I said to her that although everywhere I go men flock around me I would not think of becoming involved with any of them. To be honest now I'm not even sure that she would get anyone as she is very old-fashioned in her dress and does not even have a pair of wedges. I do be ashamed sometimes going out with her.

So I don't know now what is going to happen, she is going to phone Mary-Anne and make arrangements. I don't know whether I should tell the priest although she never goes to Mass, but I could tell him that too. If she did go to Mass she might not be having all these crazy ideas. I wouldn't tell Mr. D at all though, he's very cross and he has said many times that he does not like her going around with me, which is only jealousy like. Who would want their wife going round with me, me being a magnet for men. But I can't help that, that's the way God made me. Poor Marilyn Monroe had the same problem.

If Mrs. D does decide now to carry on with her plan would Jerry be able to come over and do some surgery on her, to improve her chances like. Tell him to bring some Botox for me that is all I need. He can make arrangements with some one of the hospitals here to give him what he needs. He could do the work on Mary-Anne when he was here too, save him another journey later on.
Love Mammy

To: Pearse@hotmail.com
Cc: Deirdre@aol.com ; Kay@hotmail.com;
From: Mammy@ eirecom.ie
May 11th

Dear Pearse
Well son, brace yourself, I have very bad news for you. Xavier and his little friend Dec won't be coming to Australia after all. Dec was refused a visa because he was involved in an incident where firearms were used when he was 18 and apparently the Aussies are very strict about that sort of thing. The incident was to do with a costume being sent from America but the whole episode is on record and the Australians are funny about records. You would think they wouldn't mind in light of their own history, but there you are now. Xavier said he did not really care as he was a bit fed up of Dec and was having second thoughts about touring the world with him anyway. I'm relieved too, a fella who was involved with guns could be very bad company.

I know now love, that it's bad news for you, but it's great news for myself and Daddy too I would think. I know you would have been looking forward to hanging around with your brother as he is so handsome that you would be bound to get some of the girls he didn't want, but son you are capable of getting a nice girl by yourself. The girls were very fond of you when you lived here. If you can't find a girl, then find a good-looking friend or an ugly friend this can work both ways, girls always go out in pairs usually one plain and one good-looking, remember your sister and Tina. Anyway you will get one definitely, no problem and who knows, you could get the good looking one, individual tastes can never be accounted for. You only have to look at Beyonce. Having said that our Paul was the good-looking friend and he ended up with Nora. Anyway I would say that the plain girls would make better wives. I would not know that for certain as I am clearly not plain and I am a marvellous wife. In any case keep trying you never know your luck. God loves a trier. Such a shame about the Chinese girl, she was lovely.

Well still no MRI scan. I said to Daddy to ring Dr Nolan and have a word and Daddy said no. Daddy is very busy now as he is up and down to Dublin and Galway all the time. Timmy is with him as he has still not gone back to work and his hair is perfectly acceptable now so he could be back . I am going to pop down to the convent to tell them that he is fit to be back at work and should not be gallivanting around Ireland with Daddy. He is still staying here too. I told Daddy to send him home as Daddy is fully recovered now but Daddy and Marie said that he can stay for as long as he wants to. Marie goes with them too as she has a student rail-card, sometimes they stay overnight or even the weekend.

Marie has an average looking new boyfriend his name is Adam and he lives down in Blackrock near Julie and the butcher. He is in a band and goes to UCC too. He is taking her to her Debs in July. She is supposed to wear a long white dress, that is the tradition but she said she is wearing a backless black dress like a ballet tutu with over-the- knee striped socks and Converse boots with twine for laces. She will be a holy show and Sister Angela has already phoned me to ask what she is wearing. I had to say I didn't know.

Adam said he is wearing your father's old army uniform which will be a sight as Adam is 6 foot 2 and Daddy is only 5 foot 7. He is wearing that with a slashed tee-shirt with a dickey bow and striped socks to match Marie's. He is also wearing Jesus sandals. It won't surprise me if the two of them are arrested. Personally I think Marie is rebelling against me as I have always been an extremely stylish person. I said to Marie won't you be able to see her underwear under the tutu and she said that it's not a problem as she won't be wearing any. So now what do you think of that? I said that I would tell Daddy but I couldn't discuss her underwear with him. He would not have a clue.

This heat wave is killing me, I am sick to my stomach with it.
Love Mammy

To: Deirdre@aol.com
Cc: Pearse@hotmail.com ; Kay@hotmail.com;
From: Mammy@ eirecom.ie
May 15th

Dear Deirdre

There's war going on here, you would think
George W and Tony Blair were in the house, not
that I would have let either of them past my front
door like. Although I suppose if they thought at
the time that I had weapons of Mass Destruction
on the property there would have been no way of
stopping them.

Anyway the trouble started when I suggested to
Timmy that it was about time that he went home
as his Mammy must be missing him in her own
way. He said I was right and he would go up and
tell her that he was coming home so she could get
his room ready and get the groceries and the beer
in and you know sort things out in general.

He had been gone about an hour when his car
screeched up outside, if Paul was here he would
have arrested him. He came in and his face was
bright red. I asked him what was the matter and
he said and I quote, 'that f!@*ing Russian
ba!@*#d,(that fucking Russian bastard) he's taken
Mammy away from me, have you got a knife, I'm
going back up there to stab him'. I said 'there's a
set of Sabatier knives in there on the work-top'.
Through my psychology studies I know that it's
best not to take any notice of men as they are

always looking for attention. Of course Daddy had to interfere and ran into the kitchen and took the knives from him and said 'Timmy boy, sit down there now and calm down'. He told me to give him a brandy. I said we had no brandy but he found it and he got Timmy a glass and one for himself. I said to Daddy 'where is mine, I am in a state of shock due to Timmy's behaviour '. Well Timmy said he was a bit calmer now and we should go down to the pub to talk about it and to get him away from the knives. Off we went anyway and to cut a long story short he said when he got home that the Russian was sitting in his (Timmy's) recliner watching his DVD of 'Home Alone' using his DVD player and his 50-inch LCD TV and listening to the dialogue on his surround sound system. I said I thought that his mother had bought the home-cinema system including the TV and the DVD player and he said yes she had, but that technically they were his as he would get them in his mother's will. Timmy said his mother told him that she had given up her 5 jobs because the Russian said he would pay for everything as a man should and she need no longer work her fingers to the bone. Timmy addressing his mother said 'what time is he going home at as I am going to be moving back in later on today'. Mary-Anne said 'well he won't be going home actually, this is his home now'. Timmy asked her if the Russian was sleeping in his room and Mary-Anne said 'well he is and so am I, we have moved your stuff into your old room because the box room was a bit small for the two of us.

Timmy said he ran up the stairs and it was true all his stuff was in the box room and only a single bed as his king-size bed would not fit in there. Timmy asked where was his bed and Mary-Anne said they had given it to charity as the Russian thought it would be better for them to have a new bed for themselves. Timmy said that that was bad enough but when he went into his gym, (the middle bedroom) it was all cleared out and turned into a home-office. I said to Timmy 'never mind, you never used the gym anyway, that was a waste of space' but he said he had been planning to use it every day once he went home. To be honest now though I always thought that Mary-Anne should have had the middle bedroom and she had paid for all that gym equipment anyway so I had no sympathy for Timmy there.

Mary-Anne then told Timmy that if and when he moved back in that he would have to start pulling his (not inconsiderable) weight. She would not be getting up at 6am to get his packed-lunch ready (he likes his sandwiches to be made on the day that he eats them and not on the night before as they would not taste as fresh), she would not be making him a full cooked breakfast and going to the shop to get him a newspaper (he doesn't like them being put through the letterbox as sometimes they can get creased). She would not be doing his washing and ironing anymore either but she would show him how to use the washing machine and would direct him to the nearest dry cleaners. She also said that as herself and the Russian would be eating out a lot more he should probably learn how to cook (I don't know why she said that as Timmy is a great cook, he was making lovely meals here) and that when she did the cooking he would have to do the washing-up. She would not be staying up anymore to cook him a meal when he got home from the pub or club, that he should get a take-away on the way home. Mary-Anne said as well that he was the father of six children and therefore old enough to buy his own clothes and that he was lucky that Julie takes so little money from him to bring up the children and he was getting away with murder with the amount he gave her each week.

Timmy said that he was feeling awful at that point but the main shock had not yet been revealed. The main shock was that Mary-Anne said that herself and the Russian had decided that Timmy would have to pay board and lodgings from now on. When he was telling us that he broke down, he said 'I need all my wages for myself and I never had to pay board and lodgings before and I certainly don't intend to now, how could I manage to go out every night and to the match on Saturdays and Sundays if I have to pay board and lodgings to live in my own house'. I said I thought that his mother owned the house and he said technically it was his as it would go to him in the will. He blames it all on the Russian, he said himself and Mary-Anne had had a lovely life till the Russian came on the scene and now he was ruining everything. So the situation now is that Timmy has given Mary-Anne an ultimatum, him or the Russian. I don't know who Mary-Anne will choose.

Daddy said then that Timmy could stay at our house for as long as he needed to. Well, on reflection I'm not too happy about that but by that time I had had several peach-brandies, which I thought was a peach-fruit drink but it was not and I felt extremely benevolent towards Timmy and agreed with Daddy. I will chat with Daddy about it when they get back from Dublin. No wonder I have an aversion to alcohol, it would get you into terrible trouble I'd say.
Love Mammy

To: Pearse@hotmail.com
Cc: Deirdre@aol.com ; Kay@hotmail.com;
From: Mammy@ eirecom.ie
May 16th

Hello Children,
Well things are not going too well here at all.
Timmy is now officially 'homeless'. That means
that he has nowhere to live. He is distraught and it
is pitiful really a man of his age. I spoke to Mary-
Anne and she said he can come home anytime he
wants but that she cannot and will not live in her
spare room anymore. Mary-Anne was at pains to
point out that much as she loved her child she felt
that at 32 with six children he should have moved
out of home a long time ago and that she felt it
was now time to have a bit of a life herself. I said
to her that he was going to move out when his
third child was born and Julie got a place of her
own but that he had to stay at home due to her
(Mary-Anne's) nerves. She said that her nerves
were much improved now and that Timmy was
only 22 then and a bit young to be moving out. I
said 'shur Xavier is older than Timmy and he is
still at home, although I know that Xavier's
situation is different as he has no kids and is
applying himself to choosing the best education
that Ireland has to offer'. There was no talking to
her though, her mind is made up. The Russian is
staying.

I told Timmy what his mother had said and he said that under no circumstances will he move back in as long as the Russian is still living there. I asked him what would he do so and again Daddy said he can stay here for as long as he wants to. I told Daddy then that we were to have a summit meeting in the kitchen tonight at 8.30 and that only the immediate family members could attend so Timmy and Mr. Ahern were not invited. Of course, all of this is Daddy's fault if he had not been so lazy on that snowy morning and took the bags out to the car one at a time none of this would have happened. Instead in his rush he was taking 4 bags when he slipped on the ice and got the broken ankle and then Timmy had to move in to help with him, I could not be looking after him on my own, not with my conditions. Daddy took the lazy man's load carrying 4 bags at a time in the snow and ice. I am going to mention this tonight at the summit meeting. I have rang Paul and asked him if he wanted to attend and he said no, he was working. I said could he not get some time off but he said he could not. I said can I use his vote then and he said that while he had no idea what I was talking about I could do what I liked as I usually did. His attitude was appalling. I have a good mind to tell Nora what he said about her Easter dinner.

I am going out now to buy some snacks for the meeting and some sticky labels that we can use as name badges as this is a very official meeting

whose outcome will affect us all. Remember that
Timmy is using a room that one of you might need
at some point.   I will email later on to let ye all
know where we stand.
Love Mammy

To: Deirdre@aol.com
Cc: Pearse@hotmail.com ; Kay@hotmail.com;
From: Mammy@ eirecom.ie
May 16th

Dear Deirdre
I am addressing you as you were the only one to
bother to email me back and express your
concerns regarding the Timmy situation. While I
did not like the tone of your email at least you
bothered to reply. I really don't see why you feel I
should let Timmy stay with us. I am not his mother
and I have the six of you to think about which is
more than enough thank you very much. Perhaps
Timmy would be better off moving away from Cork
altogether and living in London. As you are so
concerned with his welfare I will mention to him
that he can go and live with you and Gary in the
micro-flat.

The summit meeting was a disaster. Nobody,
not even Xavier, would wear their name badges.
Marie said it was a stupid idea as we all know
each other only too well. I pointed out that certain
protocol had to be followed during official
meetings. I said that George Bush and Tony Blair
clearly know each other and they wear name tags
at meetings. Marie said 'have you never heard the
saying, best to say nothing and be thought a fool
than say something and confirm it beyond all
doubt'. Daddy actually sniggered until I gave him
my look and then he said 'Marie apologise to your

mother, that was uncalled for'. She said sorry but in a way that made me feel that she was not sorry at all.

I called order and said that we were here to discuss what was to be done about Timmy. I said that while I liked Timmy (and I do) it was clear that he could not live with us as we were overcrowded already and he is very fat. Daddy said 'he's doing no harm in the spare room'. I said I needed the spare room as I was sure one of ye would move home at some point. Yourself being the most likely when you finally realise that you could marry a successful Irish boy. Marie said she liked Timmy staying here as he cooked lovely dinners. I said to Daddy 'obviously you love Timmy staying here as he has yourself and Mr. Ahern like alcoholics down the pub every night'. Daddy said that it was I who had asked Timmy to stay in the first place and that that gave Mary-Anne the chance to go out and meet the Russian. I pointed out to Daddy that it was his fault that he had slipped on the snow and broke his ankle. Daddy said that Xavier and his pal should have taken their own bags to the car. I said 'so you are saying it would have been better if Xavier had broken his ankle'? Daddy said he was not saying that but that if Xavier had broken his ankle then I would have looked after him myself. I said 'who else would be expected look after him but his own mother'? Marie said 'who would be expected to look after Daddy but his own wife'. I was horrified. How on earth would I find the time to look after Daddy with a broken ankle when I have a busy and varied life outside the home, not to mention my health. While I have devoted my life to Daddy and my children I am still a modern, independent woman.

I said that I felt we were getting nowhere and that we should eat the snacks and calm down. No-one wanted to eat the snacks as Timmy had made a beef stew for dinner. I said in that case we could take a vote as to whether or not Timmy could stay and as I had Paul's permission to use his vote I was voting no twice. Daddy and Marie voted yes, no surprise there, but then Xavier abstained. So there was a hung jury. Daddy said that Timmy could stay for the time being and that was the end of that .

I was in a state of shock as Xavier never lets me down. In fact I am still reeling from the whole thing and I am phoning the doctor to come out and treat me for shock and I don't even care if it's Dr Nolan or not.

Love Mammy

To: Kay@hotmail.com
Cc: Deirdre@aol.com ; Pearse@hotmail.com
From: Mammy@ eirecom.ie
May 17th

Dear Kay

Thank you for your email and I knew that you would side with Timmy as you two were always the very best of friends growing up. Perhaps I should suggest to him that he should go and live with yourself and Jerry in New York where he could hang out with the likes of Jennifer Lopez and Lady Gaga. Get over yourself girl.

The doctor came last night and he was a lovely little African man and when I told him all my troubles he said 'family can be a blessing or a curse and clearly, dear lady, yours are a curse'. He was appalled at the abuse I suffered and offered to put me into a rest-home for a while - which I declined. I told him, if I went into rest-home now you would not know who they would have moved in when I came home. He said I was making the wisest choice as your father had no right to move his homosexual partner Timmy into the family home. I had forgotten to mention that Timmy was Daddy's nephew and I think some of my story got a bit mixed up due to the language barrier. He advised me to call the police and I said Paul was in the police and was one of them too. He said he was shocked that there were homosexuals in the police. He thought that I could go to the Priest and when I told him none of them went to Mass he said he was not at all surprised to hear it. He said if I wished he could get a priest from his own religion to call in and have a chat and perhaps remove all the bad spirits from the house. I said he could if he liked and then he gave me a few valium. I know that the doctor got a bit mixed up but he was so nice that I did not want to embarrass him by correcting his assumptions. I asked him did he know Daddy and he said no so that was ok. The he also gave me some sleeping tablets and I did not even wake up when they got back from the pub.

I think now the only solution is to for you three to come over here and I can call another surprise meeting and then we can vote again. Would you be able to get over next week at all?

I did mention to Timmy this morning that it was all Daddy's fault that he was homeless but he said he did not blame anyone but the Russian who had brainwashed his poor mother.

Timmy is gone back to work now with the nuns so at least he is not hanging around the house all day or running around the country with Daddy. Xavier said he was sorry if I felt he had let me down but he liked Timmy being here as he drove him anywhere he wanted to go and bought him a pint every night. Xavier is a sensitive soul. It seems to me that (apart from Xavier) no-one cares about the pressures this will put on my relationship

with Daddy and if I end up in the singles club with Mary-Anne and Mrs. D then you all have only yourselves to blame. If you are all to be damaged by coming from a broken home then so be it.   I am in two minds whether or not I will continue to sacrifice everything by devoting myself to Daddy and my children or whether I should go off and get a Russian for myself.
Love Mammy

To: Pearse@hotmail.com
Cc: Deirdre@aol.com ; Kay@hotmail.com;
From: Mammy@ eirecom.ie
May 19th

Dear Pearse

Once again I find myself to be the blameless
victim. I did not say that Daddy had moved his
homosexual partner Timmy into the house I know
that Timmy is Daddy's nephew. I thought that the
doctor knew that, so when he said about the
homosexual lover I did not want to embarrass him
by correcting him, after all he is a doctor and a
very nice one at that. And also he is a stranger in
a strange land. He does not even know Daddy or
Timmy so there is no harm done and doctors have
to uphold an oath of confidentiality so he can
hardly talk about it with other patients or his peers.

    Now is there any chance that Timmy could join
the Australian police? He is a very good cook and
he can drive and he often drives to work straight
from the pub so he is reliable and not one to be
taking days off with a hangover. Also he is on
first-name terms with most of the Garda in the
local station so he does get on well with the police
types.   I would phone and ask your boss myself
but I don't feel able to due to the previous mix up
about the lottery win and his dead mother. Ask
him when you see him and let me know.   Timmy
is a bit overweight but the police man in 'Home
and Away' is no slim Jim.

Timmy could move in with you and ye would have a great time going out on the town and you would be the handsome one in that group of two. Think about it now, he would make your dinner every day as well. He could change your life for the better. His personal hygiene beyond question, he always has a shower when you tell him.

You won't believe this but I met your old buddy, Kevin, this morning down Shandon Street. He has moved back home from America because he got offered a great job at Apple Computers. As you know Apple's European Operations Headquarters is here and Kevin will be heading-up some part of it. Who would have thought it. I always thought he would end up in prison and that he was a bad influence on you but now look at him and in a way it was yourself that ended up involved with prisons as you spend a lot of time with criminal types. He said he is buying a big house out in Bishopstown and I asked him if he will be moving his mammy in but he said no that she was happy enough where she was. Anyway I invited him up for dinner one evening when Timmy will be cooking and he said he would love to come. He asked me about you and I told him you were still in the same small apartment with no girlfriend and wearing that causal Australian type clothing. He had on lovely expensive jeans and a designer jacket. He said I

had not aged a day and I said I know but thanks anyway. He is a handsome lad and I told him to keep away from Mary-Anne as she was mad for the young fellas now.

Paul and Nora are gone to Dublin today with the kids to go to Nora's brother's wedding. Unfortunately Nora's granny died last night so it's all very uncertain now. Well it's certain that there'll be a funeral but they don't know about the wedding. The poor woman was in hospital for months and was on tubes to be fed and everything. Paul's son Eoin went to see her two weeks ago and popped/shoved 4 chocolate peanuts into her mouth. The woman had been 'nil by mouth' for months. Whether or not that had anything to do with her demise is uncertain. Paul said the doctor said definitely not, but you would have to wonder.

Are you thinking of coming over at all for the summer? Let me know so I can start airing the spare room. I might re-decorate it in fact. It was only done for Xmas but with Timmy being in there for the last few weeks it's looking a bit the worse for wear.

Love Mammy

To: Deirdre@aol.com
Cc: Pearse@hotmail.com ; Kay@hotmail.com;
From: Mammy@ eirecom.ie
May 22nd

Dear Deirdre
Well some good news at last. Nora is having a single birth. They were not too sure with the first scan but it's certain now. To be honest I don't know how they make anything out on those scans. I had 34 when I was expecting Marie and all I could see was snow like when the television is broken. Thanks be to God anyway that it is only one baby, two sets of twins is enough for anyone. Especially when they are all hyper. Nora's mother was supposed to be looking after them when Paul and Nora went for the scan but she was not feeling too good, (she is a hypochondriac definitely) there was something gone amiss with her diabetes and she was taken into hospital and Paul rang me at the last minute and said 'are you doing anything today'? I thought he was going to take me to lunch so I said no and then he caught me and said 'I'll drop the kids down when we are going to the hospital for the scan and we will also visit Nora's mother when we're there'. What could I say? I quickly removed anything breakable, took up all the rugs and removed the cushion covers. Then I asked Daddy if he could mind the kids and he said no he was going to work. Marie just

laughed at me and Xavier was busy upstairs studying on the Internet. Timmy was at work at the convent and when I rang his mobile he did not answer so I was stuck.

When Paul got here I asked him could the children not go with them as it would be lovely for them to see their granny and he said after the peanut incident he felt it was best to keep them out of hospitals for a while.

Well in they came and I told them to sit on the sofa and be good. I asked them if they want to watch a video of Daniel O' Dolan but they did not. They wanted to watch some other channel on the television, and I gave Ciaran the remote as he is the oldest. He put on 'The Jerry Springer Show' so I took the remote immediately. What on earth do those kids be looking at, no wonder they are hyper. Marie came down and said they would play a game of 'hide and seek'. Well it was mayhem in the house. They were upstairs disturbing Xavier's studying and screaming and laughing and running and shouting. Then when Marie had to go they wanted me to play. I said I would so I told them to go and hide. Of course I did not go looking for them, I sat down and watched Jerry Springer and they were grand and quiet hiding for the next half hour. They wised up after a while though and came back downstairs. They said they were hungry and I asked them what they would have for lunch and they said cookies and Cola. So I gave them that and they seemed to be even more hyper after that. I will have to speak to Nora about their diet.

Luckily for me Mrs. D called in and she sent them outside in the yard and told them to do some gardening. I told her all about the Timmy situation and about the African doctor and how he had made incorrect assumptions but she was only laughing and it is funny no matter what Pearse thinks. Mrs. D said she wanted to chat with me about her marriage problems but Paul and Nora arrived and told us the good news about the single child and then they rounded up the other four, who were covered in mud and smelled funny, and off they went.

By that time Mrs. D had to leave as she had to go to town so I don't know what she wanted to tell me. We are going out for a meal tomorrow night so I will let you know.
Love Mammy

To: Kay@hotmail.com
Cc: Deirdre@aol.com ; Pearse@hotmail.com
From: Mammy@ eirecom.ie
May 23rd

Dear All

I am just emailing to remind you that it is Xavier's birthday on June 10th. DO NOT FORGET ABOUT IT. He will be 33, can you believe that my firstborn will be 33. I can remember vividly the day he was born. It was a glorious sunny Sunday and he was the easiest birth of the six. I had got up early in the morning and had a bath and washed my hair. I put on my white maternity dress and then Daddy made breakfast and we sat outside in the garden and I felt a little pinch. I said to Daddy 'I think it's time dear'. Daddy got the suitcase and started the car and off we went to the hospital and the doctor there was amazed at my composure as the baby was ready to be born. I said 'oh' and there he was, smiling up at us. Daddy was waiting outside, and then he came in and he was in tears. It was truly like something from a film. Actually Xavier was the easiest one of all of ye in every way, he never gave me a moment's trouble. I had my figure back before I left the hospital as Xavier was only 6lbs and not a big heifer like the rest of ye. Even the other new mothers in the hospital agreed with me when I said that he was the best looking baby there.

Anyway enough reminiscing, the point is that he has had a tough old time being on the dole so I want his birthday to be lovely for him. So here is a list of presents that he would like.

1. Cash in €50/£50 note denomination as he does not like small notes American or Australian dollars.
2. Rolex watch (I am getting this)
3. All inclusive week in Cancun for two (he couldn't go on his own after all).
4. 50 inch LCD TV.
5. Shopping weekend in Paris for two (he couldn't go on his own).
6. All inclusive trip to Las Vegas to see Celine Dion.
7. Gucci The G Chrono with Diamonds (another watch for evening wear)
8. Flying lessons.

So there you are now you have plenty of choice. I am getting him the Rolex and a new laptop and as an extra surprise I have arranged a weekend away in London for himself and his new little friend, Antonio. So Dee be prepared they will be over the weekend after his birthday. You know the drill ha ha. We are all going out on the night of his birthday for a meal at the Ramada Hotel in Blarney. You are welcome to come if you can get home but as none of you could get home for the meeting regarding Timmy I'm not really hopeful that you can make the birthday.

Well I must be off to get ready for my night out with Mrs. D.

Oh by the way don't forget that Paul's twins are making their First Communion this weekend.
Love Mammy

To: Kay@hotmail.com
Cc: Deirdre@aol.com ; Pearse@hotmail.com
From: Mammy@ eirecom.ie
May 25th

Dear Kay

I am not feeling well at all and I haven't changed any of my habits so I really don't know what is wrong.

I went out for a lovely meal with Mrs. D the night before last. You won't believe this but I fell for the non-alcoholic wine trick again. I had drank ten or twelve glasses when I said to her 'I'd swear I'm a bit merry'. She started laughing and said 'you are, it's real wine not the non-alcoholic one'. Well we laughed and the waiter was amazed that I fell for it again. He said he thinks I should start drinking properly but I told him I took the pledge when I made my Confirmation and have only ever drank by accident or for medicinal purposes since then. I am intentionally a tee-totaller forever but there have been mistakes I must admit. Mrs. D said then 'God love her and she's been drunk at least once a week for the past 20 years'. The feckin cheek of her, she's nearly an alcoholic herself like.

Well Mrs. D is going ahead with her plan to have an affair. Now I have advised her but in the end I am not the boss of her. She is going out with Mary-Anne and the Russian this weekend to a dance down town. She is going shopping tomorrow for something to wear and I am going with her to advise. As you know I am considered to be a stylish, elegant woman.

I had a bit of an uncomfortable experience today. I went to my appointment with Dr Nolan and I must say that when I went in Dr Nolan seemed much calmer than of late. He said 'I have been reading your notes after Dr Bernard paid you a home visit. Had I been aware of your family situation, I could have offered yourself and your husband some counselling and support'. I said 'What in God's name are you talking about, I'm here about getting my MRI scan'? He then said that Dr Bernard had 'flagged' the fact that Daddy had moved his homosexual partner into the family home. I nearly died. I had to explain that the little African doctor had got mixed up somehow and tell him the story about Timmy. Girl, he gave me a big lecture about people's reputations being ruined through spiteful jokes. I had no idea what he was talking about, shur I don't have a spiteful bone in my body, and told him so. It was clearly a misunderstanding on the part of the doctor and therefore it was nothing whatsoever to do with me. I also said to him that even if Daddy were homosexual why would that ruin his reputation, that got him. I said Doctors were not supposed to make judgments on peoples' sexuality and then I walked out with my head held high. I also completely forgot about the MRI scan so will have to make another appointment now.

Still though if Daddy found out that there was even a hint of scandal he would not be very happy. It's lucky the doctor can't tell him. They are sworn to confidentiality.

How are things in New York are you still friends with Jennifer Lopez?

Love Mammy

To: Pearse@hotmail.com
Cc: Deirdre@aol.com ; Kay@hotmail.com;
From: Mammy@ eirecom.ie
May 26th

Dear Children
Oh, Jaysus the secret is out. I will never again talk
to a doctor especially an African one.

We were all sitting down to eat the lovely meal
Timmy had cooked, our first barbeque of the year,
Paul and the kids were here and so were Mr & Mrs
D and the Aherns. Next thing we heard all the
commotion outside and I went out to answer the
door. There was a big American man dressed all
in white standing there with a bible in his hand.
He was shouting 'God cleanse this house of
fornication, sinners come out'. I said 'who are you'
Daddy ran out and said 'what is going on'? He
said 'Dr Bernard has sent me to clear this house of
the Devil'. The neighbours came out then so I
rushed us all inside. I had to practically drag him
in as it seemed to me he liked an audience. We
got in and Daddy said 'now what is going on
here'? The American said 'Leviticus 20:13 If a
man also lie with mankind, as he lieth with a
woman, both of them have committed an
abomination: they shall surely be put to death;
their blood shall be upon them'. I looked at poor
Xavier and his face was green, he got an awful
shock as you know how sensitive he is. By this
time Daddy was practically foaming at the mouth

114

and grabbed the American by the collar. The American said 'unhand me sinner, you brought your homosexual lover Timmy into your family home and you will rot in Hell'. Then he put his arm around me and said 'for the pain you have caused this beautiful woman you will be punished'. Daddy shouted 'take your hands off my wife you madman'. The American hit Daddy with the bible and Daddy landed him a punch on the chin that floored him. It all happened in seconds but the punch calmed things down and Paul said he would call in his colleagues and then I knew things had gone too far and calling the guards would only make matters worse so I had to tell the truth.

The big American was all apologies to Daddy and then he said to me that I would be damned in Hell for ruining my husband's good name. At that Timmy threw him out. Would you believe he knocked on the door again and asked if we needed any counselling, he only charged €150 per hour. This time Timmy caught him by the belt and collar and ran him out the gate. He won't be back.

Well Daddy was none too pleased, as you can imagine. In fact I had never seen him so angry and especially not with me. Timmy and Paul were laughing but not when Daddy was looking. Daddy lectured me for a good half an hour and then they all went down to the pub and left me at home to 'think about what I had done'. The bloody cheek of him, you'd think I was a child. I didn't spend any time thinking about it I went into town with

Mrs. D and we got two lovely outfit's and new shoes. Hers for her night out and mine for the twins' Communion tomorrow.

When Daddy came home he said 'we'll say no more about it now, but Timmy can stay as long as he likes'.

I was kind of stuck there without a leg to stand on and had to agree.

Love Mammy

To: Pearse@hotmail.com
Cc: Deirdre@aol.com ; Kay@hotmail.com;
From: Mammy@ eirecom.ie
May 27th

Dear All

Things have gone from bad to worse here. I will start at the beginning to set the scene.

We all got ready to go to the twins' Communion and I must say that I looked a vision of elegance in my new outfit. I said to Daddy, 'it's true what the American said though, I am a beautiful woman'. Daddy said 'I thought we were never going to mention that again'. You couldn't get a compliment from that fella.

The ceremony went well and the twins were very well behaved, (under threat of no Communion money from Paul). They all looked lovely, even Nora, although she is the size of a whale with this baby.

Well after the ceremony we went home and then we were all planning to meet up later for a meal down town. I was glad to get home as the new shoes were killing me. Daddy volunteered to take the younger twins home with us as they were not well behaved because obviously there was no Communion money to threaten them with.

I went for a lie down and when I got up they were all down stairs drinking beer, including the twins. They had a can of lager each. I said to

Daddy 'what are you doing giving them lager'. He said 'shur one can is no harm'. They were enjoying it anyway and it was keeping them quiet and they fell asleep soon after so no harm done.

At 6 we went off down to meet up with the others. Nora's family was there as well. Good looking they are not. We had a lovely meal and everyone had a few drinks and then Daddy invited them all back to our house for more drinks.

There we were all drinking and chatting and then Paul asked Ciaran and Eoin how they had enjoyed their Communion and they said it was great they had €400 each to spend tomorrow. They wanted to buy plane tickets to go to America to see Jerry Springer but Paul said no. Then Daddy asked them to sing a song and Ciaran sang some football song but then Eoin said he wanted to say a poem he had made up himself. Himself and Ciaran were in stitches laughing so I was hoping it was not going to be rude.

Oh my God. Rude would have been so much better.

He stood in the middle of everyone and Daddy called for order and Eoin began;
'Granddad and Timmy sitting in a tree,
Doing something they shouldn't be,
It starts with S and ends in X,
Oh my God they're having sex'.

You could have heard a pin drop. I didn't know where to look, Nora's family were stunned as was ours.

There was nothing else for it but to explain the whole situation to them as well. They were laughing like but Daddy was not. He was certainly not seeing the funny side at all.

Instead Daddy was incensed – again. He said the whole of Cork will be talking about him and then he had the cheek to blame me. It did not enter his head at all at any point that it was all his fault for breaking his bloody ankle in the first place. I am raging, I make one little error of judgement during all my years of marriage and this is how I am treated.

To be honest now I am not happy at all with the whole situation. I have spent my whole life waiting hand and foot on my family and all I get is the blame for every little thing that goes wrong.

I said to Marie, 'as you know I am not given to histrionics but I feel like I could die'. She said 'if you do can I have your stuff'.

I am thinking of leaving your father and Marie and taking Xavier and moving to Hollywood and opening an elegant and stylish shop for the stars. Who knows I might be discovered by a Hollywood scout for the parts that Michelle Pfeiffer usually plays.
Love Mammy

To: Kay@hotmail.com
Cc: Deirdre@aol.com ; Pearse@hotmail.com
From: Mammy@ eirecom.ie
May 28th

Dear All

I thought I'd better keep you up-to-date with the Daddy situation. He is still not happy, in no way can he be described as happy, and is acting very coldly towards myself which I don't like at all. I hate an atmosphere, unless it's a good atmosphere obviously.

How on earth Daddy can think that I had anything to do with all the homosexual stuff is beyond me. He is acting as if I did something wrong where I clearly did not. In fact he is so livid that 'me thinks he doth protest too much'. Perhaps he is homosexual and I stumbled upon his secret quite by accident whilst in the execution of one of my good deeds. What do you lot think?

Could I be right? I'd say I could. However, I don't want to jump to conclusions as that is not my style at all. I spoke to Xavier about it but he seems strangely reluctant to discuss it with me which is unusual as normally he loves 'discussing' Daddy but only for the craic like, he's fond of Daddy really. As am I, I'm fond of him too.

It all fits really now that I think about it. I am the perfect trophy-wife so Daddy could use that to hide his true sexual-orientation. To be fair there are things that don't fit too though, his personal hygiene is not the best and he has no sense of style whatsoever. He would wear, and often has, stuff from the Charity shops. His hair is not immaculately groomed either, he will not dye it blonde like Sting or have a few highlights no matter what I tell him. He does not own one designer piece and his swimming trunks are down to his knees, definitely not Speedos. He drinks pints and has never ordered a cocktail, not even on holiday. He does not love Cher or Madonna or Liza but he does like that one who is the athlete, you know the runner and she does look like a man. In musical terms he likes the Dubliners and the Pogues, and God knows none of them are exactly gay icons, and he actually commented that 'Frankie Goes to Hollywood 'should f off and stay there where they belong'. He has never shown an interest in Interior Design and hardly notices when I have the place decorated. He thought Feng Shui was a meal from the Chinese takeaway. He does have a lot of male friends though but not one of them looks gay. Then again he does go to the gym, he says it's to keep fit but he would say that. His regular pub is The Harp and Shamrock and that is an awful dump, it certainly does not scream sophistication or style and no self-respecting homosexual would go in there to use the toilet never mind have a drink. You have to bring a towel to sit on if you care about your clothes.

Daddy does not wear any jewellery and nearly had a heart attack when Xavier got his various piercings done. He does not have any tattoos although I did once draw a moustache on him when he was drunk and being as his hygiene level is now only medium and was then minimum, he went up to the army the next day with the marker moustache on and no-one told him till his CO called him in. However, I digress and am getting away from the clues.

Still now though I think it all points to a secret life. It would be an awful shock to me but of course I will stand by him It happens to all the stars. There's the reason now why he never bought me that pink diamond, I suppose he would have loved it for himself. I also understand now why Daddy is being so cold towards me, I suppose he looks at me and thinks 'there she is that beautiful (in mind as well as body) woman and I cannot be the man she wants'. Shur that would break anyone's heart.

So there you are now children, your father is gay. I hope you will not think any less of Daddy as he can't help it, it's just the way that he is. As for me, shur I will try to carry on but as you know Daddy is the love of my life and I expect all sexual relations will now have to be cancelled for the time being. I suppose I could always get a nice young man to fulfil my sexual needs but that would not go down too well with the Church and the neighbours.

Neither will the fact that Daddy is a gay but it would explain why he never goes to Mass.

He is away now on a courier job in Dublin but I will confront him when he comes back tomorrow. When I say confront I mean in a gentle, understanding way. I can just see the relief on his face when he realizes that he no longer has to live a lie and that I will support him through the ordeal of rehab. That is what happens as far as I know. There has to be some sort of cure for husbands who are gay, Kay you will have to explain that to me as though I have vast medical knowledge I am a stranger in a strange land when it comes to the ways of the homosexual.
Love Mammy

To: Deirdre@aol.com
Cc: Pearse@hotmail.com ; Kay@hotmail.com;
From: Mammy@ eirecom.ie
May 28th

Dear All
Well I have never had 3 replies from the 3 of you
on the same day before and definitely never as
quick either. You are all very concerned about my
marriage. I don't know whether to be pleased or
tell you to mind your own business and to
concentrate on your own relationships, or lack of
one in your case Pearse.

I am rather thrown off balance that you are all
so quick to dismiss the case that I have outlined
pointing to Daddy's homosexuality. So what if he
has six kids, so have I, that does not mean that I
could not be gay although obviously I am not. The
Yorkshire Ripper had no children and that did not
stop him being a serial killer.

Pearse I am disappointed with you in particular.
You are a policeman albeit in the Australian police
force but even so. I would expect you to look at all
the evidence impartially, as they do in CSI. If the
CSI New York team were here they would weigh
up all the evidence and have the whole thing
sorted out in an hour. Your reply saying that
Daddy is in no way, shape or form a homosexual
arrived so quickly I really don't think you have
taken the time to look at the evidence I outlined. If
that is the way you handle the cases in Australia

124

then it's no surprise that your boss would not let Timmy join the force. He probably thinks Timmy would be as incompetent as you. I am not saying you are incompetent now like as I am not one to jump to conclusions. Also the way that you said that Daddy was not homosexual implied that there would be something wrong with him if he were. I would have thought that as a policeman that you would have been far more PC and not judged people on their sexual orientation. In fact it made me wonder if you were hiding something yourself. You have no girlfriend, although like your father you are not stylish or perfectly groomed. Perhaps you would like to consider going homosexual. I'd say that Australian men would not be very fussy at all. Even if you could not get a man it would do wonders for your appearance.

Looking at you, Paul and Daddy I really don't know where Xavier got his sense of style from, well I do know but modesty prevents me from saying so. So Pearse make your mind up now boy gay or straight, it's up to you. I won't mind either way as long as you are happy. Give it a try anyway you never know.

Anyway Deirdre and Kay I am also taking into account your rapid responses frantically denying any homosexuality on Daddy's part and so will not confront him tomorrow about it as you all seem to think it would be a bad idea and might make

Daddy even crosser than he is already. I suppose I was being a bit premature advising Johnny Depp that I was soon to be single although he had every right to know under the circumstances and he is Xavier's no.1 choice for stepfather. Don't tell Daddy as he is madly jealous of Johnny Depp and always says he is a Queenie.

I am nearly demented from Mrs. D sending me texts. I have not had time to look at them as I am going through a crisis myself but the constant buzzing is very annoying when I am watching Shark Men. I have no interest in sharks but the men are very interesting.

I'm still not feeling well at all.

Love Mammy

To: Deirdre@aol.com
Cc: Pearse@hotmail.com ; Kay@hotmail.com;
From: Mammy@ eirecom.ie
May 30th

Dear Deirdre

Mrs. D has an awful secret and I am sworn to
secrecy and promised I would not tell anyone but
you are family and as you live in London who
would you tell? Well the secret is that she went
out with Mary-Anne and the Russian and she wore
all her new clothes and she danced with a fella. A
slow dance and he touched her bottom she did not
know if that was an accident or whether he was
copping a feel, the former I'd say. Can you
believe that? She said she really enjoyed it and
she is going again next week, she has no shame
or remorse. She said loads of people said she
looked like Madonna but I think they said
Maradonna, have you see him lately he is a big fat
git. In case you don't know he was a footballer
who apparently made England lose some football
tournament. Not that they were going to win
anyway like but you know how they love to whinge
and I am not going to get into the whole 'Hand of
God' thing here although Maradonna was a
Catholic so make up your own mind whose side
God was on.

I cannot imagine anyone saying that Mrs. D
looks like Madonna, people always say that

Marilyn Monroe and Debbie Harry looked like me and that is true although neither of them had that innocent modesty that I have and my beauty is all natural, if you know what I mean.

Anyway I am very disturbed by her having all that male attention, even if they do think she looks like a footballer, this could turn her head and make her question her marriage vows to Mr. D. He is an awful boring, cross man I have to say. All he does is read the paper and watch Irish language programmes on TV regardless of the fact that he can't speak a word of Irish. Nevertheless he wants Mrs. D to go on an 'Irish Language Only Holiday' in the summer. Mrs. D wants them to go to Ibiza with Mary-Anne and the Russian.

Mrs. D now is paying the price for devoting her life to her husband and children, although I have done the same, I have always kept up my own interests too and that is why I am starting a course is Philosophy next month. I think I could add a lot to the current understanding of the world.

I am off to town now with Mrs. D and Mary-Anne; we are buying some new outfits, them for their clubbing, me for my night out with Daddy. He has some army re-union or other, I can't wait… yawwwwn.

Love Mammy

To: Kay@hotmail.com
Cc: Deirdre@aol.com ; Pearse@hotmail.com
From: Mammy@ eirecom.ie
May 31st

Dear Kay

Well as usual it's all go here. Xavier said he no longer wants to be called Xavier as nobody pronounces Xavier properly. Apparently it is supposed to be pronounced Have-e-ear. That is the true Latino way of saying it. Shur how would we know that not being Latino like. Daddy is livid (again) saying there is no way that he is paying one cent towards Xavier changing his name as last time it cost him over €3000 due to Xavier having to travel around South America to research names which he thought would suit him. I said to Xavier what would you like to be called now and he said it's pronounced He-zues. He said that he would like to go to the Bahamas to research it for a few months. I said is it He-zues a Bahamian name then and he said no but the weather is lovely there. I said that sounds nice and I am sure once you get back we can all learn to say it properly. Then Daddy said 'tell your mother how that is pronounced'. Xavier said, 'it doesn't matter how it's pronounced, it's how it's spelt that matters'. Daddy said again 'tell your mother how that is pronounced'. Xavier said he'd tell me later as he was going out then Daddy said 'it's pronounced Jesus'. Jesus shur you can't name yourself Jesus, ah that's not allowed now at all. I said to Xavier 'is that true'? He said 'yes it is but you must admit it's very unusual'. I said 'unusual or not you are not calling yourself Jesus, choose some other name or stay as you are, or better still go back to Seamus the name you were given on your birth certificate'. I also told him that if he persisted with this that he would have to move out. I know now that I was a bit harsh but there is no way that I would want him to call himself Jesus, people would think he had an awful cheek, and there are some people who would think that he was the 'Second Coming'. I mean as you all know I would rather eat my own liver than have Xavier/Seamus living outside of the family home but I had to do it for his own good. He did not go out after that, he went upstairs to his bedroom and I could hear him sobbing till late into the night. While my heart was breaking I could not move my position on this for his own good as much as anything else.

There is no point in any of you now taking his side on this either. I know how you all look up to your big brother and feel like you should protect him but really now do not encourage him in this. I am very serious.

Love Mammy

To: Pearse@hotmail.com
Cc: Deirdre@aol.com ; Kay@hotmail.com;
From: Mammy@ eirecom.ie
June 2nd

Dear Pearse

How are you out there in Australia? Now as you know I am not one to pry or as the Blood and Crypts say 'not one to be all up in your business' (the twins told me that) but on the other hand I am your mother and of course I want to know what is going on in your life. Have you got a new girlfriend, you should be well over the Chinese one by now.

Surely there must be a girl over there that would be suitable as a wife for you. You are 25 and a 1992 study in the British Medical Journal found that men in Western countries today have less than half the sperm production their grandfathers had at the same age. The report examined 61 separate studies of sperm count in men in many countries, including the U.S. and I'd say Australia too, and concluded that there has been a 42% decrease in average sperm count, from 113 million per millilitre (ml) to 66 million per ml, since 1940. (There are 4.5 millilitres in a teaspoon).Furthermore, the average volume of semen diminished from 3.4 ml to 2.75 ml, a 20% loss since 1940. Thus the average man has lost 53% of sperm production in the last 50 years.

Now Pearse, that was published in 1992 so I'd say by now that it's 79%. Therefore it is of the utmost importance that you get married and have children immediately. As you know we are a small country with a small population so we do need Irish children.

I understand that you are not very interested in your personal appearance and that is your own business but really a nice suit and shirt and tie would go a long way when you are out of an evening. I'd say that no girl would be interested in that surfer boy look on you, it would be fine for Xavier as he could carry it off but then again, as you know, he can carry off any look. Anyway, are you allowed to wear your uniform going out socially as most girls do love a man in uniform, even a policeman. Now it may well be that there is a girl that you like but you can't get up the courage to ask her out, if that is the case get me her address or email and I will write to her and tell her what a lovely boy you are and ask her out on your behalf.

If there really are no girls out there then perhaps you should come home as I am sure you would have no trouble getting a nice girl here. Mary Sullivan down the road is still single, I know she is a few years older than you but she is doing really well now that they have got her medication adjusted and all the charges against her have been dropped. Also she is on the list for a stomach stapling operation so she will be grand after that.   If I were you I would make my move now before she has her pick of the men after the op.

In the meantime to keep your own sperm safe, always wear boxers not thongs or panties. Do not have sex either alone or with a girl unless you are planning to have a baby, in effect save up your sperm, I'd say the more you have the more chance you have of having multiple births and I have always wanted photos of sextuplets around the house. Also keep away from laptops and prostitutes.

So how is your job going? Are you working on any exciting cases? I believe crime is rife in Australia or is that America, well one of them anyway. Crime is not rife in Cork, as far as I know, shur Paul spends most of his working time asleep on the couch, or playing computer games once he is properly rested and can concentrate so would you not be better off coming home and working here. Are you in line for any promotion over there? You have been there for 4 years now so I would expect some movement upwards shortly. Do you have a gun, I hope not. I don't mind a Taser stun gun as that is a less-than-lethal-force but a gun is dangerous as a bigger boy could take it from you and then you might have to pay for it and I'd say guns are expensive. I think guns encourage guns, look at the yanks, the babies in

prams have guns there.

Anyway things are going along fine here. Marie is looking forward to her Debs although the nuns are not as they are worried about what Marie will wear and I have already told you her outfit plans in detail. I told the nuns that I had no idea what she would be wearing as I don't want to be involved in any unpleasantness. Now Marie is a great student but she is a bit of a rebel and really she is Daddy's responsibility as she won't listen to a word I say.

She has no intention of going on to University after school, although I got her prospectuses from colleges in Australia, Canada, America and Taiwan. She said she is taking a gap year and when I said that she could not as she would be wasting her time she had the cheek to say that Xavier had been on a 17 year gap and she would do what she likes and of course Daddy backed her up. Do they have women police in Australia, could you ask your boss if Marie could join, tell him she would terrify any criminal into surrender.

Love Mammy

To: Kay@hotmail.com
Cc: Deirdre@aol.com ; Pearse@hotmail.com
From: Mammy@ eirecom.ie
June 2nd

DEAR ALL
URGENT FOR IMMEDIATE ACTION.

DO NOT FORGET XAVIER'S BIRTHDAY HE
WILL BE 33 ON JUNE 10TH. HE HAS A VERY
HARD LIFE BEING ON THE DOLE SO PLEASE
REMEMBER THOSE LESS FORTUNATE THAN
YOURSELVES. ENCLOSED FOR YOUR
CONVIENIENCE A LIST PREPARED BY THE
BOY HIMSELF WITH A COUPLE OF
SUGGESTIONS FROM ME ADDED.

- Cash in €50/£50 note denomination as he does not like small notes or US or Australian dollars.
- Rolex watch (I am getting this)
- All inclusive week in Cancun for two (he couldn't go on his own after all).
- 50 inch LCD TV.
- Shopping weekend in Paris for two (he couldn't go on his own).
- All inclusive trip to Las Vegas to see Celine Dion.
- Gucci The G Chrono with Diamonds (another watch)
- Flying lessons

Love Mammy

To: Deirdre@aol.com
Cc: Pearse@hotmail.com ; Kay@hotmail.com;
From: Mammy@ eirecom.ie
June 4th

Dear Deirdre

Thanks for your email. Things are grand now
again, I have actually forgotten all about the
homosexual mix-up and am as happy as ever. On
the other hand Daddy is still not very happy as
somehow the story got out and all the men down
the pub clubbed together and bought him a man-
bag. It was only a joke like but he was very
annoyed. With me though not with them, how
does that work? I don't know. I just put my iPod
on and ignored him while he was ranting and
raving walking up and down the living room with
his man-bag over his shoulder. The men had
stitched it onto his jacket for the craic.

The son formerly called Xavier said he would
use the bag for carrying his passport and personal
papers when himself and his new friend Petey go
to Cancun next month. He is a very stylish person
and would not be at all embarrassed by carrying a
man-bag. He is perfectly at home with his
masculinity unlike some I could mention.

Well now D, I have noticed that you hardly
mention Gary at all these days. Are things ok with
you two? I know he's not much of a catch but
bearing in mind you have already had three

broken relationships I think that you might do well to try to make this one work. As I don't know the exact nature of the problem I will find it difficult to give you advice but I will give some general tips for keeping your man.

1. Always tell your partner how you are feeling when they have upset or annoyed you. Keeping things to yourself only make matters worse. If your partner wants to tell you their problems tell them to put it in writing so you can address it when you have the time. Otherwise they would drive you mad whining on and on.

2. Never ask your partner about their day at work , (not applicable to you as Gary has never worked a day in his life but he might work in the future, stranger things have happened) you are only making a rod for your own back pretending to be interested in their work.

3. Never cook a meal for a man (unless it's your brother). He will only eat it and expect the same the next day. Well maybe not the same meal but a meal nevertheless and then you will be cooking for the length of the relationship or until you die.

4. Never go shopping with a man. They will rush you around and complain and then think that you owe them something (i.e. favours of a sexual or gastronomic nature). Men can be handy for grocery shopping,

carrying the bags, although a taxi-man can do that just as well really. But if you choose to get your man to carry the bags meet him outside the shops as it's no business of his how much the shopping costs.

5. Never discuss your financial position with a man. Always tell him you earn less than you do and that things cost more than they actually do so you can keep the difference and buy a few nice thing for yourself.

6. Never buy an item of clothing for a man. If you do it suddenly becomes your responsibility when it comes to doing the laundry. I fell for that in the early days of my marriage and now I have to do Daddy's washing although he does all the ironing except Xavier's whose clothes I iron myself as he expects a higher standard of pressing than Daddy provides.

7. As soon as you meet a man tell him you are allergic to all types of household cleaners so that much as you'd like to you cannot take part in any household duties. That way he can either employ a maid (like Tina's husband has) or he can do it himself.

8. Always use sex to get what you want. After all if you were not having sex with him he would have to pay a loose woman so he is not losing out by giving you your own way.

Now those tips are simple but effective. I only wish someone had told them to me years ago and I would have had a much easier life overall. Although I would add that Daddy probably thinks he has the perfect wife in me and he has.

Oh by the way, I believe Daniel O' Dolan will be playing here again in August and I did tell you I would buy you a ticket. Do you still want to come, as I don't want to spend €10 and then you not turn up. Xavier, Petey, Mrs D and myself cannot wait. Love Mammy

To: Deirdre@aol.com
Cc: Pearse@hotmail.com ; Kay@hotmail.com;
From: Mammy@ eirecom.ie
June 5th

Dear Deirdre
What is the matter with you? I was not meaning to
insult you at all, why would I want to insult my own
daughter? Is your pain not my pain?   I merely
pointed out your past history with relationships.
And I beg to differ you did have three failed
relationships.

    1. The last one was with the boy you met at
       university who you 'shared' a flat with. I
       was not born yesterday and I knew that you
       were living together. Why else would you
       bring him home during the Xmas holidays
       that time when himself and Xavier were out
       on the town the whole time. You did your
       best to hide that fact you were very peeved
       that the lads got on so well but as your
       mother I could see it clearly and I must say
       now that at the time I did think it was very
       selfish of you as you had him all the year
       round and Xavier was only being friendly. I
       actually mentioned it to Daddy and he said
       that you seemed in great form to him but
       what would he know about romance. When
       you finished university you telling me that
       you did not split up, that ye had never been

141

a couple, and that he was gay didn't fool me. Had he been gay I would have spotted it a mile off. I have a great affinity with gay men.

2. The second one was Patrick Murray who broke your heart as I recall. I know that he did not drown on purpose and it was not his fault that the dinghy got taken out to sea, or was it? Did you ever think that perhaps he might have sailed off to America or somewhere to begin a new life. There is a young film star that is the image of him and he is from Cork, Jonathon Rhys-Myers or something. Where would a fella from Cork get a name like that? Anyway something to think about that Patrick may have staged his disappearance not that actor fella's name.

3. Then there was the lovely Martin, your first love. I know that his family moved to Australia but he was 12, he could surely have got a little flat and a part-time job if he had really wanted to stay. He never did write either. I wonder where he is now, do you want me to ask Pearse to trace him. There are not that many people in Australia surely. He could be a doctor now or a lawyer or even an accountant

I'll ask Pearse to send out an APB like they do on CSI.

Actually I will ask him now. Pearse can you get on that stat. Deirdre could be married before ˎ Xmas.
Love Mammy

To: Kay@hotmail.com
Cc: Deirdre@aol.com ; Pearse@hotmail.com
From: Mammy@ eirecom.ie
June 9th

Dear Kay

How is New York, New York so good they named
it twice? More importantly how is the lovely
surgeon Jerry and yourself too like. Things are
well here and we are all looking forward to
Xavier's birthday. Deirdre's present and Pearse's
have arrived already so yours must be on the way.
It should be here tomorrow. For future reference
post your presents earlier rather than later as poor
Xavier so looks forward to getting presents and as
you know, (well happily for you, you would not
know - you are one of the lucky ones) Xavier has a
tough enough oul life on the dole.

   I am just waiting to wake him up; he had a late
night and told me not to wake him till the afternoon
as he needs his sleep to look his best. When he
gets up we are going out to lunch and then
shopping in town. I am buying him a new outfit to
wear for his birthday and a new outfit for myself as
well like as I haven't got a thing to wear.

   Tomorrow we are having a pampering day. I
have booked the Presidential Spa a superior
Health Spa here in Cork. We are having all the
treatments they have to offer, money no object, I
will use my credit card. Xavier is really looking
forward to the 'Time for Men' Facial which is very

144

reasonable at only €100. We are both having the 'Absolute Deep Tissue Ritual' at under €200 each followed by the Exotic Frangipani Body Nourish Wrap. We are also having eye-treatments, pedicures, manicures and waxing. Neither of us needs the treatments, obviously, but it is nice to be pampered on your birthday.

Well I will finish this later as it's almost time to wake the birthday boy up so I must go and squeeze some oranges and separate the eggs for his egg-white omelette.

Here I am again. It's 2 o' clock in the morning and we just got in. I know you are all anxiously waiting for the blow-by-blow details of the Birthday Eve but it's the actual big day now. We got our outfits. I got a beautiful red satin dress with a big bow on the hip, I also got some Christian Loubuitton shoes, and a bit of costume jewellery. Xavier got some Rock and Republic jeans for the day and a Valentino suit for the evening. The shopping was exhausting so we decided to go for some light refreshments, well what I thought were light refreshments but Xavier forgot that I don't have Tequila in my Margaritas and after a few of them I was very hungry and a little unsteady on my feet. We phoned Daddy and asked him to come and collect us but the phone rang alright at first but then we could only get an engaged tone so we had to get a taxi back. Both Daddy's and

Timmy's mobiles were on charge. We stopped at the all-night café and got burgers and chips.

Well goodnight all, I am off for my beauty sleep. Don't forget to ring your brother later to say 'Happy Birthday'.

Love Mammy

To: Pearse@hotmail.com
Cc: Deirdre@aol.com ; Kay@hotmail.com;
From: Mammy@ eirecom.ie
June 11th

Dear All

Well yesterday was a mixed bag really. It started off badly as I was not well at all, my head was pounding and I felt sick to my stomach it must have been that burger and chips.

Staying out all night was a mistake as I had planned to wait for Xavier to go to bed and then blow up the balloons and put up the decorations. I had wrapped his presents but wanted to have them all laid out outside his bedroom. The main presents from Daddy and I were the Rolex and the Cancun trip which is actually for a fortnight as it's a long flight and they would hardly be there before it was time to come home had it only been for a week. I had bought him a few other little things as well, a remote control car, cologne, a Mont Blanc fountain pen, Calvin's, diamond cuff links and little things like that just to open.

I thought Daddy would have bought something personal too but he did not, isn't that awful though that he would not even think to buy his eldest son a little gift. He is not thoughtful at all. When it was Daddy's birthday last week Xavier gave him a lovely Pine air freshener for the car. Well I got it as a free gift and gave it to Xavier for his own car but no, being the kind and thoughtful boy he is he asked me to wrap it up and gave it to Daddy. He also hand-made a card and although I don't like to get anything home-made (unless it's made in a top designer's home) and I do prefer shop-bought the card was lovely and Xavier had written a lovely message in it. There was a little mix-up - he did forget to sign it and Daddy thought at first it was from Ciaran and Eoin so that upset Xavier first off and he took back the air-freshener and that annoyed Daddy so I had to time-out both of them. I told Daddy to read the card again and say thanks and recognize Xavier's efforts. Here is the message he wrote, you could call it a poem really.

'All the best

Have a good rest'.

He spent his time composing that and he is not even a poet although he could be as I am rather poetic myself. I say 'rather poetic' as modesty forbids me from going into more detail.

So back to today. I did get up at 5 but I was not in the mood really due to burger and chips making me sick and Daddy would not get up and help with the preparations. Timmy was going to work at 7 but it takes him well over an hour to make his hair presentable, he is a feckin eejit that boy. The hair has grown upwards and outwards instead of down since the burning incident and no amount of gel or wax will tame it, so he was no help at all. Marie was at Adam's in spite of me telling her to be at home to sing 'Happy Birthday'.

I had to stand outside Xavier's room and sing it on my own but Xavier shouted 'shut the f**k up' and I was so shocked that I did and went back to bed.

Xavier did apologise to me when he got up, he said he thought he was having a nightmare so that's fair enough.

Kay there was no present from you; I am very disappointed so I had to tell Xavier that the diamond cufflinks were from you. I did not want him to get upset on his birthday especially as you have snubbed him twice already this year. The Jennifer Lopez affair and then not turning up in Las Vegas to meet him. Pearse, he got your 50 Australian dollars, I suppose that's worth about 20 Euro in real money. Are you sure you could afford it? Deirdre, there is no way that he would wear a jumper and especially one from a chain store. It is exactly the same as I got Gary for Xmas, has Gary worn his yet? Can you send me a photo of him wearing it with today's newspaper held in his hand and the date clearly displayed, just as a matter of interest.

So after Xavier bravely put the disappointment with the presents behind him we had a Bucks Fizz breakfast. I had to have a few glasses on a special day and in any case Bucks Fizz is not alcohol at all hardly, a drop of champagne never hurt anyone. We also had smoked salmon and scrambled eggs for breakfast. Daddy took too long going for our magazines and everything was gone when he got back. He made himself some tea and toast before driving us to the hotel. I told him we could have hired a limo but he would not allow it being the spoilsport that he is. To be honest I did not think in time to book it anyway. I think the hotel should provide a limo really; I will write and advise them.

Well the treatments were fantastic, really now we were pampered like the special people we are and the food was lovely too. All the girls were in love with Xavier but I told them he had to concentrate on his career before he thought of relationships. Shur they were only laughing at me. I did ask Xavier if he had chosen his university yet and he said that the only one he liked this year was in America, but University College Cork might be doing the same course next year so I told him to wait till then. I'd die if he went away although I would not stand in his way. I'm not that kind of mother. If he went to America I'd have to go with him, and you all know the gang situation over there, I'd be terrified that they'd be waiting to mug me.

Daddy was late picking us up and we nearly missed our hair appointments. We only just made it although Zoë said that we were cutting it fine for Xavier's highlights and lowlights, but we looked lovely when we were done.

We got a taxi out to the hotel for the meal. Neither Daddy nor Timmy wanted to be the designated drivers although I had arranged for them to be so Daddy had to pay for 5 taxis as the plan was for himself and Timmy to do multiple runs. I said Timmy should have paid half but Daddy said 'leave it woman' very crossly.

It was a lovely meal and the wine was flowing. I am worried that I am turning into an alcoholic and am starting the 'twelve step' programme next week. I will probably drink away till then as there is no point stopping now, I would not be an alcoholic then and would be wasting everyone's time going to the programme.

All the family and a few of Xavier's friends were there for the meal. The manager was giving Timmy very strange looks when he walked in. He asked Daddy if Timmy was bothering us and Daddy said 'no he is a homeless nephew of mine'. Daddy is very sarcastic. I must say though that I was ashamed of my life over the way Timmy was dressed. Xavier and all the lads were dressed gorgeous and all had their hair done and were wearing lovely cologne. Not a girlfriend amongst them, I think that is the problem with being too good looking, they have their pick of the girls and then they don't want to stay with just one. That would not explain why Timmy does not have a girlfriend. Timmy was wearing his 1990 Ireland shirt, which I'd say has not been washed since

151

1990 and Bermuda shorts that were once vibrant, probably around 1970. Then of course his hair, oh the shame.

The kids were very badly behaved as usual. They are very bold boys, the four of them. Even the smaller fellas are feckin wild. Ciaran sat down at some Italian family's table and would not come back to our own table and he was being very cheeky and eating their food and asking them who had the best soccer team Ireland or Italy. The man said Italy and Ciaran said that actually whenever these two countries have met Ireland has beaten Italy more times than Italy has beaten Ireland. How did he know that - he is only 6? Anyway the Italian man disputed it and Paul said 'are you calling my son a liar' and the manager said he was calling the police and Paul said 'do what you want' and the manager said 'sorry'? and Paul said 'you will be dude, I am the police' (I was proud of him when he said that, not that the manager would be sorry but that Paul is a guard and when he said dude, he was very NYC cop-like). Paul insisted that the manager go on the internet to check out the football history to see who had beaten who the most and as it turned out our boy was right (Paul has the list but I won't bore you with it here). Paul then told the Italian man and Ciaran to shake hands or he would arrest them both. They shook hands then and the man bought Ciaran a glass of orange which was a big mistake as orange makes them even more hyper than they usually are. When Ciaran went to sit with some German people and asked them who had the most Eurovision wins Ireland or Germany Paul decided it was time to leave.

Nora was also fooled by the non-alcoholic wine and she was drunk as a skunk. Imagine it a Ban Garda, and a 7-month pregnant Ban Garda at that, drunk. She is the size of a house, honestly now, it must be a baby elephant she is having. All I hope is that the child is not ginger. We have enough of them now 4 is enough for any one family. When Paul said they were leaving Nora said 'goodbye'. I don't know if things are great there, it's the stress of all them foxy children. Once Paul and the kids left Nora really let her hair down and she was sitting on Timmy's knee half the night. She must be blind like, Xavier had some lovely friends there and she was sitting on Timmy's knee. Still it stopped Timmy from glaring at the Russian all night. We did sit them at opposite ends of the table but the tension was fierce. Mary-Anne had a few vodkas and attempted to try to make the peace by buying them both a drink but she fell off her platforms and had to be taken home early. However, the Russian very generously paid for the meal and drinks. Daddy was delighted and the Russian was considered a friend for that night anyway.

Once the meal was finished then we all decided to go to town and the lads wanted to go to a place called 'Ruby's' I'd never been there as I am not much of clubber but I asked Daddy if he wanted to go and he said 'no'. I said I would go anyway but Xavier said that I'd better not as he was not going. He said he was just going to the chipper and would be home after that. I was surprised at that as we had only just had a huge meal and he usually watches his calorie intake but it was his birthday and I suppose his metabolic system was hyper.

I went home with Daddy and Timmy, and Xavier and Nora and the lads went to town. I was glad Nora went; in case of any trouble it is always handy to have a garda with you. I got the cake ready with the candles lit for when Xavier got back but he was still not in by 1 and so I rang his mobile phone and he said that the chipper was packed so for me to go to bed and not to worry myself. There was very loud music in the background, I suppose they put that on so that the customers would have something to listen to while they were waiting for their chips.

Oh Deirdre with all the excitement I almost forgot Xavier and Petey will arrive in London at 12 noon tomorrow. Make sure Gary gets to Gatwick early. Don't worry too much about lunch a nice lobster salad with warm bread will be grand.
Love Mammy

To: Deirdre@aol.com
From: Mammy@ eirecom.ie
June 12th

Deirdre
What in the name of God is going on, where are
you? We are all in an awful state here. Xavier is
totally traumatized, he had to be sedated at
Gatwick Airport earlier and Daddy is now on his
way over to get him to bring him home. He is
being held by the airport police in Gatwick. Timmy
is taking me out to the airport now to meet them.
God help us all.
Love Mammy

To: Deirdre@aol.com
Cc: Pearse@hotmail.com ; Kay@hotmail.com;
From: Mammy@ eirecom.ie
June 12th

Dear Deirdre
Where are you? I have been phoning your little
flat and your mobile phone all day. I am worried
sick. Your mobile is dead; I hope you're not dead
but if you're not I will be very interested to hear
your explanation as to why your brother is nearly
ready for committal to the mental institution.

They went off lovely this morning with Daddy to
the airport, no mishaps. I shed a little tear but I
knew he'd be home in 4 days, Xavier not Daddy.
Daddy came home and was just getting the lunch
ready when the phone rang. Even the ring
sounded urgent, I knew there was something
wrong. Daddy shouted 'answer the phone' but
there was no-one else here so he had to come in
and get it himself. His face went purple and he
was saying 'alright, ok, sorry about that, no there's
no need for that you can just send him home'. He
hung up and I said 'what's wrong, is Timmy down
with the guards again'? He said no. He said that
he did not have time to tell me and he really did
not have the whole story but he had to go over to
Gatwick immediately to get Xavier or they were
going to commit him to an English mental hospital,

and you know what the state of the NHS over there is, Jaysus.

They are home now and here is the whole story. Daddy said that from what he could work out Xavier and Petey landed on time at Gatwick and went through customs with no problem. However, when they got to the arrival lounge there was no sign of you and/or Gary. They waited for a while anyway and then Xavier found a policeman and told him that there was no-one there to meet him. He said the policeman said 'and' and then walked away. Can you believe that 'AND' from a policeman. Imagine a guard saying that to a lost person at Cork Airport. Petey suggested they phone you but there was no answer, they tried your mobile as well but that was off. Petey said that he had friends in London that they could stay with but Xavier couldn't stay with strangers, you know he is a very private person and in any case who would wash his smalls? Anyway these friends of Petey's could have been murderers or white slave traders or anything. England is full of that sort of people I'd say. At that point Xavier began hyperventilating and then the airport security people came over. To make matters worse that Petey said he was heading off and got a bloody taxi and left Xavier there on his own. Xavier then apparently became hysterical and the security people had to take him into a room and call a doctor and get him sedated with Valium. At that point they managed to get our phone number from him and they called Daddy. They told Daddy come and get him or he would have to be committed.

When Daddy got there he said Xavier was a gibbering wreck and ran into Daddy's arms. Daddy said the security man said that perhaps he should take Xavier for psychiatric assessment, he asked Daddy if Xavier was a 'Special Needs' or 'Care in the Community' person. What a cheek, the poor boy was a stranger in a strange land, lost and alone, what would they expect, who wouldn't panic. He always makes sure that he has someone to meet him at airports, usually his little internet friends.

They have been home now a couple of hours and Dr Nolan has just left. He was very rude really and said that he thought that when I rang and said that I had a child who could not breathe that I was talking about one of Paul's children. He did not appear to be very sympathetic to Xavier's plight at all. His bedside manner leaves a lot to be desired. Poor Xavier is sitting there in a stupor breathing into a brown paper bag and Daddy appears to be in an awful temper for some reason. Still he is at home and safe now and I will look after him and nurse him back to health.
Love Mammy

To: Deirdre@aol.com
Cc: Pearse@hotmail.com ; Kay@hotmail.com;
From: Mammy@ eirecom.ie

June 12th
Dear Deirdre

I cannot tell you how I am feeling right now, I don't have words to describe it, I don't know if I have ever been so upset in all my life. I cannot believe that you went off to the seaside instead of meeting your brother. What do you mean you did not know he was coming over? I told you weeks ago he would be over the weekend after his birthday, you should have rang up and made sure you had the information.

Xavier is in an awful state and is even thinking of not going to Cancun next week. In fact he may never travel again. I hope you can live with that, travel is his only pleasure; he is on the dole after all and is very confused about what career to pursue. You on the other hand have it all. A university education, a small flat, a good job, and a partner who one day may be able to support you.

To make matters worse Xavier cannot trust his best friend Petey now so obviously Petey will not be accompanying him to Cancun and somebody will have to pay for the tickets to be changed and I think that somebody should be you. That's if Xavier decides to go at all.

What did you go to the seaside for and why did you not take your mobile phone? You have ruined

Xavier's birthday. I hope you can live with that
also. As usual it is me, your poor mother who will
have to pick up the pieces. I will be ringing around
tomorrow for advice from the top counsellors in
Cork. What will you be doing, going off to the
seaside for a day of fun I suppose.
Love Mammy

To: Kay@hotmail.com
Cc: Deirdre@aol.com ; Pearse@hotmail.com
From: Mammy@ eirecom.ie
June 15th

Dear All
Just to keep you up to date on the situation with
Xavier. He was still refusing to come out of his
bedroom this morning. Daddy went up and told
him to come out as he wanted to talk to him about
Cancun but Xavier said he did not want to talk to
anyone.

Daddy went off out then and I made Xavier's
breakfast and he left a note outside his door
ordering Caesar Salad for lunch and asking if I
could wash and iron his silk shirt for tonight. So I
did.

There was not much more I could do at home
then so I went to see Mrs. D and told her about all
the commotion caused by Deirdre. She said to me
'shur you have devoted your life to your husband
and children, you don't drink (only occasionally) or
smoke (only socially) and you hardly spend a
penny on yourself and there's the thanks you get'.
She also said 'if you were a celebrity you would
win Celebrity Mother of the Year, every year'. She
got that right she is very perceptive alright. She
said we should go out for a meal tonight and I said
we would. I said I would have a few drinks as I am
going to the 12-Step meeting next week.

Daddy came home then at about 5 and he went up to talk to Xavier about Cancun. Xavier shouted 'I cannot even contemplate Cancun at the moment leave me alone, why won't you understand I just want to be alone'. Daddy said 'not to worry boy I have solved your problems and cancelled the holiday and got the money back so now you don't have to be anxious at all, that's one of your worries taken care of'. Xavier said 'can I have the money'? Daddy said 'no you cannot and you'd better come out here as I am not prepared to talk to you through that door for another second'. Xavier said 'I never wanted to go to Cancun I want the money to go to the Bahamas to meet my internet friend'. Daddy said 'you can feck off'. I ran upstairs to see what was going on but Daddy said 'get back downstairs now, this is between me and him'. He was so cross that I did. Xavier was hysterical by then and believe it or believe it not Daddy was laughing in a cross way which is worse.

When Daddy came downstairs I asked if he had really cancelled the holiday as I thought he was trying to shock Xavier into normality. Anyway I was certain they would not give you the money back just like that. Now here is the shocker; Daddy had been to see Dr Nolan who had given him a note saying that Xavier could not travel and the company had refunded the money in full back on to the credit card.

162

Daddy and Dr Nolan have an awful cheek. Xavier might have rallied in time for the holiday with a bit of TLC but no, they took it into their own hands and made the decision for him. His birthday is well and truly ruined now. Although I had no idea he did not want to go to Cancun. I asked Daddy if I would book a trip to the Bahamas for Xavier but he said 'absolutely not, no more trips for him at my expense'. Sometimes I think Daddy does not love Xavier as much as I do. But then again how could he not, Xavier is adorable.

Deirdre I hope you are feeling as bad as you should be. Ring your brother up and apologise or he may never come to visit you again.
Love Mammy

To: Kay@hotmail.com
Cc: Deirdre@aol.com ; Pearse@hotmail.com
From: Mammy@ eirecom.ie
June 22nd

Dear Kay

Well we are of course, delighted with your news. Being invited to the 'Hamptons' is great altogether, where is that exactly, is it the seaside? I'm not too sure why you would need to think about buying a property there as you won't need it when ye move home. I suppose you could always rent it out. I will tell Xavier where you are going when he comes home, he might know where it is.

All is fine here. Xavier is battling through the disappointment of his birthday. He is gone out today with his new friend, Julian and I am relieved as he had not seen daylight since the London emergency. He was going out at night alright but only after dark. Poor child.

He said to say thanks for your present (I told him the cuff links were from me) although he does not really like watching films at all. I told him to send them back to Jerry to watch (do surgeons watch films?) but it would cost more to post it than it did to buy it.

I have written off to a television programme for Timmy to have a make-over. Honest to God now he is a disgrace and how will he ever get a girl and move in with her looking the way he does. Having said that though it's not too bad having him here,

164

he makes lovely dinners. Himself and Marie and Daddy get on famously and even Xavier likes him although Tmmy is always picking him up and throwing him over his shoulder for the craic. However, he cannot stay here forever as I need the room and he makes Daddy go to the pub most nights. Then of course when his six children come up the house is a wreck and when Paul's come at the same time, well I just have to leave the building.

So when are you two coming over for your summer hols? You did not come at Xmas so I am looking forward to seeing you soon. It would be nice if you could come for my birthday on August 18th. You could bring Jennifer Lopez if you like, Xavier would love that although she would have to stay in a hotel as I don't have room for her with Timmy being here. I could ask Mary-Anne if she could stay there but her spare room is a bit small especially if the twins come as well. Still I don't suppose they would mind sharing a single bed as it would save them up to €70 per night. You could all come to see Daniel O' Dolan on the 21st. Let me know ASAP so I can get the tickets. As you can imagine tickets for Daniel are like gold dust but I can try and being a member of the fan club I do get special treatment.

I saw that Cillian Murphy was in New York, did you meet him? I emailed his agent with your

address and told them that he could call in to see you but you did not mention his calling so perhaps you were out. I think you would have mentioned it if you had seen him as you are a bit of a name dropper, you get that from Jerry. I mean that in the nicest possible way of course.
Love Mammy

To: Pearse@hotmail.com
From: Mammy@ eirecom.ie
June 29th

Dear Pearse

Thanks for your email. It is a pity that Marie can't join your police force as I think she would fit in great out there with her drinking every night, love of rugby, and her affinity with criminals who sell weed. Mrs D told me that she saw Marie with a certain person who sells weed. I said to Mrs D is that a crime and Mrs D said she thought it was as weed is Cannabis which is a Class drug. I know what Cannabis is but I don't know what a Class drug might be and neither does Mrs D. Mrs D thinks it might be a better drug than others but I don't know. I think now that if Marie is speaking to that person (her cousin Timmy's friend) then she may be smoking Cannabis. I looked up Cannabis using on the net and have indicated the signs that are applicable to your sister. Amongst the signs are:

Dilated (large) pupils   Don't know.

Cigarette rolling papers   No

Seeds that have been cleaned from marijuana
No

Smell on clothing, in room, or in car
No

Bloodshot eyes	No
Sleepy appearance	Yes
Reduced motivation Room	Yes, won't clean her

Pipes, bongs, homemade smoking devices (you may see sticky residue from burned marijuana)
No

Anxiety	No, not a care in the world
Difficulty thinking	Not according to her exam results

Distorted sensory perceptions
Don't think so

Dry mouth	Only after cider nights
Feeling sluggish	Yes if it involveshousework

Grandiosity (acting in a pompous or boastful manner)   Always

Impaired judgment   Yes no fashion sense
Impaired short-term memory

                          Yes always forgets to
                          repay loans

Increased appetite, craving sweets
                          Yes always eating

Sensation that time is passing slowly
                          Yes always waiting for weekend

Social withdrawal and isolation
                          No

Discoloured fingers   No

Sleepiness   Yes stays in bed all
                          day.

So now, son, you are the policeman, let me know if she is a drug addict or not. If she is I will be mortified and very cross. We will have to send her to rehab. Daddy will be heartbroken. The family will be ruined.

I struggled and went to AA last night but to be honest I think I was over-reacting and am not really an alcoholic at all although the fella there was trying to persuade me that I am in denial. He was an awful eejit. I said to him 'I am not powerless over alcohol and it has not ruined my life, in fact it makes my nights out very enjoyable

indeed. I don't even really drink'. There was not one famous person there, I don't blame them. The others were all alcoholics so you can imagine going out with them it would depress you and none of them would drink. I phoned Daddy to come and get me and we all went down to the pub where I did have a few pineapple juices as one of my 5-a-day. I did have a dash of vodka in each. Daddy had told me not to go to AA as I was only wasting my time and for once he was right.
Love Mammy

To: Deirdre@aol.com
Cc: Pearse@hotmail.com ; Kay@hotmail.com;
From: Mammy@ eirecom.ie
July 12th

Dear All

Great news. I am off to Isle Capri for three weeks.
Mrs. D is taking me. Tina's husband sent the
tickets for Mr. and Mrs. D but Mr. D would not go
because they do not speak Irish over there. Tina
and hubby will be meeting us there. That is where
his family is from. We are staying at the Capri
Palace Hotel-Spa and hiring a boat with a captain
for a few days. I cannot wait. Mrs. D has assured
me that there are no gangs at all on the island, in
fact it is called the' Island of Love and Romance'.
Not that I will be looking for love or romance, I
have Daddy. Mrs. D might meet someone though.

It's all a bit sudden, but Mrs. D did not want to
tell me in case the tickets could not be changed.
We are going on the 19th the day after Marie's
Debs so that fits in nicely. I don't think I would
have gone if it meant missing the Debs as I would
never have heard the end of it.

I went to an advanced Philosophy class but
found that while I could perfectly understand that
'Sartre, along with Albert Camus and Simone de
Beauvoir, all represented an avowedly atheistic
branch of existentialism, which is now more
closely associated with their ideas of nausea,
contingency, bad faith, and the absurd than with

Kierkegaard's spiritual angst. Nevertheless, the focus on the individual human being, responsible before the universe for the authenticity of his or her existence, is common to all these thinkers', I understood all that perfectly and in fact had some ideas that would illuminate it all but Icould not pronounce existentialism so that was the end of that. It's a shame really as I feel I could have brought some new ideas into the debate and it is highly likely that I would have become well know as a worldwide influence in philosophical thinking. A Nobel Peace Prize would not have been beyond the realms of imagination. Also the woman who was teaching the class seemed a bit spacey to me. She was wearing an Aran sweater and tweed pants. I mean style is important if you want to make a statement so the statement she was making was 'I'm a bit of mess'. She said 'if a tree falls in the forest and no-one is around to hear it does it still make a sound'. I said 'who cares' she said 'that is a whole other question' I said 'this is a load of rubbish, I want my money back' she said 'you would have to speak to the admin about that'. I said 'I will be speaking to the Head of the College about you. He is a personal friend'. He's not like but best to keep these people in their place. I mean what a bloody stupid question. In the first place who would know if the tree had fallen and who would know if anyone had been there or not except the person who was there or not. Who would know when a tree had fallen anyway unless

172

count as there would be animals at least in the forest. It's a load of garbage and your one is making money for nothing.

I was very reassured Pearse that you think that Marie is not a drug person. Thanks for your professional opinion on that. All my sacrifices for your educations were worth it.
Love Mammy

To: Pearse@hotmail.com
Cc: Deirdre@aol.com ; Kay@hotmail.com;
From: Mammy@ eirecom.ie
July 18th

Dear All

Marie has just left for the Debs in a limo. Xavier
was all excited helping her to get ready. He has
recovered from the London incident now. He did
tell me that he had not wanted to go to Cancun
this year as there had been terrible storms there a
couple of years ago and he was frightened that he
might be blown away in a hurricane but he did not
want to hurt my feelings by saying so. He had
been to Cancun before and loved it, he met lots of
Hip-hop boys there and they had a great time.
Shur I just assumed that he would have liked to go
back there but apparently it is no longer so stylish
since half of it was blown away. So really it was
all my fault. Xavier said that had he not had the
stress of having to go to Cancun to contend with
he would have coped much better with Deirdre not
turning up at the airport but really it was a cry for
help. He asked me to intervene and get Daddy to
spend the money on a trip to the Bahamas. I said
I will.

   Anyway back to Marie. They looked lovely,
both of them. Marie did not wear her planned
outfit. She wore a gorgeous dress, it was black
though, not white, and she did wear the Converse

boots but somehow she got it right. It must be having such a stylish mother. Adam did not wear Daddy's old uniform, he wore a suit, it was white though not black but he looked very Pierce Brosnan. Instead of a flower he bought her a bottle of cider which was thoughtful. They are not allowed to drink at all at the actual do, it is policed by the nuns but they were meeting up with some friends in a pub in town before hand and then eating mints to hide the smell of alcohol.

I have to tell you all that Daddy was not as pleased about my holiday to the Isle of Capri as I would have expected. He was very put out in fact. He said 'I asked you to go to Italy and you said you would not'. I said 'well I wouldn't go to Italy ' and he said 'but you are going to Italy'. I nearly died, I had no idea that I was going to Italy, I thought I was going to an Island near Jersey. I did not let Daddy know that though, he thinks I am a very stylish woman of the world and I would not want to spoil that impression. In any case I did not want to go away on my own with Daddy in case he thought it was an opportunity for sexual activity. As ye know I am having a terrible time with the menopause. You know men are always looking for the ride. Still I may have hurt his feelings but wherever you go there you are and I am his wife not his mother.

Then Xavier was none too happy either. He said I was being selfish going off on a holiday when he could not go to the Bahamas. He said could he come with us but Mrs. D said no. She said boys like him might not be accepted by the locals. I'm not quite sure what she meant by 'boys like him' although I suppose the locals would see him and, as they say in the magazines, all the girls would want him and all the boys would want to be him and there would be great jealousy which could cause tensions between the Irish and the Italians as if there is not enough tension already due to Ireland being the better football team and rugby team. Daddy then got cross with Xavier and said 'your mother deserves a holiday on her own if she wants one'. Talk about confusing signals, one minute he is raging because I am going, the next minute he is raging because Xavier is raging that I am going. They do not seem to be getting on at all and I am the poor fool who is stuck in the middle. I will be glad to get away.

I am a bit nervous now although I asked Paul to ring Interpol to confirm that there is no gang activity in Capri. Paul said he did and there is not. He was able to confirm that in the five minutes between me asking him and me calling him back to check although he was interviewing a shoplifter at the time. I'd say he is very powerful in World Police circles. But no matter how powerful he is he wouldn't tell you a bit about who was being interviewed for what crime. Mrs. Duggan's son was arrested for being drunk and disorderly and I did not know a thing about it till I read it in the Echo. What use is having a son in the Garda if you have to read about your neighbours' shame in the paper?

So now, I will be away for the next 3 weeks so ye will all have to solve your own problems, keep your own counsel and cry on someone else's shoulder. I know ye will miss me and I will miss ye too but it is time that I had a holiday after the stress of this year so far. Be sure to ring Daddy regularly as he seems a bit cross.
Love Mammy

To: Kay@hotmail.com
Cc: Deirdre@aol.com ; Pearse@hotmail.com
From: Mammy@ eirecom.ie
August 1st

Dear All
Well here I am home again. I could have emailed from Italy, they have the Internet there too. Who knew?

We had an absolute ball. Although I was sick a few times but that is foreign water for you. Capri is such a beautiful place and I would love to go back there again although with Daddy this time. The weather was glorious the food was excellent. The shopping was great although they expect you to watch while they make your sandals but I would have no interest in that sort of thing. I don't care how they are made as long as they are stylish.

The people are very nice, for Italians, and there was no gang activity as far as I could see. I was looking. I really cannot praise Capri highly enough. Dom (Tina's hubby) hired a boat with a captain and we went all around the Gulf of Naples and the Amalfi coast! Mrs. D was weak for the captain, he looked like Al Pacino, in his younger days now like, I'd say had it not been for Tina's presence there might have been a romance there. They did get lost one evening when we went to eat in Ischia, another Island. They were missing for a good two hours. What happened was they were walking up behind us and we took a turning and they took the turning after us although Dom had said that there was not another turning but there must have been. I said to Dom that we could look for them after dinner, I was starving. In the end they turned up just as we were finishing our food. Mrs. D was a bit flustered and there was all bit's of straw and twigs on the back of her top and in the back of her hair. The captain was a bit mussed up as well. She had fallen down a hill God love her the captain had to rescue her. It's those platforms, she is as bad as Mary-Anne.

So I had a great time but I did miss you all and Daddy too. I did not bring back any presents as my credit card did not work over there for some reason so I had to budget my spending money but Dom paid for everything anyway so I did manage to buy a few nice dresses for myself and some Italian shoes for Xavier.

Tina is a credit to her mother and she is beautiful. Her hair, nails, skin, everything shines. She has had her teeth done in the American way; I'd say Xavier would love his like that. Tina treats her mother like a queen. She is very respectful towards her and never once raised her voice or called her mother a feckin eejit. Isn't that lovely.

The only little cloud was Dom's family. Now there is no doubt that they have loads of money but I found them a bit rough. They are constantly on mobiles and shouting Vafanculo whatever that means. Of course they were all staring at me and half of them were in love with me I'd say. Italian women are not very fashionable so I was a novelty.   I had to keep putting my hand on my face to show my wedding ring. I'd imagine they would hop into bed with you at the drop of a hat, Catholic or no.   In any case we only met them twice so it wasn't too bad.

I was delighted to see Daddy at the airport although I found him a bit cool. I think he was jealous of my tan and new white dress with matching sandals. Had I known it was lashing rain with gale force winds I would have re-thought my outfit.

When I got home then the holiday was well and truly over. The house was filthy, there were tea-stains in the cups. The washing was piled up to the ceiling, someone had spilled red wine on my white rug and there was crayon drawing all over the walls. There was hair in the shower and a tide mark on the bath. Timmy was wearing the same top he'd had on when I left and I would not be surprised to learn he had not changed it since. They were all there, Daddy, Marie, Xavier and Timmy. I told them that I was shocked at the state of the house and I was going to bed and wanted it back to normal by the time I got up. Xavier said 'can we have our presents before you go to bed' and he loved his shoes. Marie was not so keen on her key-ring with the Isle of Capri on it.   I gave

Daddy his lighter but he instead of saying thanks he said 'so you expect me to take up smoking so'. Timmy was delighted with his lighter.

So I went off to bed and slept till now. They are all gone out so I have no news apart from the holiday. I will write later when I catch up with what has been going on.

A phone call from each of ye would not go amiss and I was disappointed to see that there were no emails in my inbox this morning. Mrs. D had flowers from Tina waiting when she got home although Daddy had to give her a lift from the Airport as Mr. D has gone on holiday to the Gaeltacht on Cape Clear. I don't know why he is going there as he cannot speak a word of Irish. Feckin eejit.

Love Mammy

To: Deirdre@aol.com
Cc: Pearse@hotmail.com ; Kay@hotmail.com;
From: Mammy@ eirecom.ie
August 7th

Dear Deirdre
Thanks for your email. I am so sorry that I was away in your time of need. I did have my mobile but no charger so I was stuck there. I knew that Gary was no good and when I got your email saying that it's over my first thought was 'she's better off without him'. What happened? Did he leave you for another woman or indeed another man? I thought he had his eye on Daddy at Xmas. Is he married and leading a double life? Did he get a job and decide he could strike out on his own now? Did you not use the tips I gave you?

You poor child you must be in an awful state. I would say that I know how you feel but I would be lying as I have never been dumped in my life. I always ended things and left a trail of broken hearts behind me. Daddy always says 'she left a trail of broken hearts behind her, but she stayed with me and broke my brain and bank balance too'. He says that messin like. Daddy knows how lucky he is.

Now the thing is that I don't like to think of you over there on your own pining for Gary. I think you should come home immediately. You can easily get a job in a school here as you did your training here and it is time you put something back into the Irish economy.

Email me immediately and let me know all the details. I will phone you tonight.
Love Mammy

To: Deirdre@aol.com
Cc: Pearse@hotmail.com ; Kay@hotmail.com;
From: Mammy@ eirecom.ie
August 9th

Dear Deirdre

I am still reeling from our phone call. And no I do not have an Italian accent, and even if I do I was there for three weeks.

Anyway I am stunned that you broke up with Gary. I cannot believe that you were seeing someone else. Who is this Omar anyway. Is he Irish? Is he Catholic? Omar Sharif is from a Catholic family but I don't think he is Irish. It's not him is it? It had better not be, he is way too old for you, if it is break it off this instant.

I would be grateful if you could send me the following information by return;

1. Who is Omar?
2. When and where did you meet him?
3. How old is he?
4. What nationality is he?
5. Is he stylish?
6. How tall is he?
7. Where does he work?
8. Where does he live, at home with parents, alone or with friends?

Also can you send me his bank statements for the last five years. You don't have to send the originals, just scan them in and email them.

How did Gary find out, was he upset? Where is he now?

Email me back immediately now as this is very important. I am feeling a little out of control with all this happening. I never knew you were a cheater. Still I suppose it's better that you did it to Gary than he did it to you.

Oh I suppose you all know but the Debs went very well, Daddy said it went off without a hitch. Love Mammy

To: Deirdre@aol.com
Cc: Pearse@hotmail.com ; Kay@hotmail.com;
From: Mammy@ eirecom.ie
August 10th

Dear Deirdre

You don't need to worry about telling me where
Gary is, he's here. He arrived last night in an
awful state and Daddy and Timmy took him down
to the pub so I have only just spoken to him.

The boy is heartbroken, he cannot believe what
you have done. He gave me all the details and
said you were waiting for me to go to Capri to
make your move. He said he had suspicions for
some time as you were way too happy but he was
busy concentrating on his studies and did not
really pick up on the clues. The clues included
you going to the seaside in June and staying
overnight. Other clues included you buying new
underwear and wearing make-up. But the main
clue was that Omar was constantly sitting next to
you on the couch watching TV while holding your
hand. Gary thought he was your gay friend and as
he felt secure in his ability to keep you happy he
did not question things he should have. He said
that sexually things had died down a bit, but I told
him that I really did not want to get into that.
Eewww.

He told me Omar is Asian, is he Chinese? That
would be great as you and Pearse can chat about

186

interracial relationships between Irish and Chinese people. Is China in Asia? To be honest I don't know where is what these days. When I went to school (and that's not too long ago) there were five continents, and the four seasons were completely different with Autum beginning in August. These days Turkey and Greece are European and countries I have never heard of are in the Eurovision Song Contest.

Anyway back to the matter in hand.   I told Daddy, Gary cannot stay here. We don't even know him, he is not family. I told Daddy to tell him to go home to his own parents. When Daddy approached it Gary begged him to let him stay for a few days as he feels closer to you through us. So what could we do?

Anyway I am still waiting for answers to my questions.

Love Mammy

To: Deirdre@aol.com
Cc: Pearse@hotmail.com ; Kay@hotmail.com;
From: Mammy@ eirecom.ie
August 15th

Dear Deirdre

This is gone beyond a joke now. Gary is crying 24/7 and he is getting fatter by the minute. Please take him back. He is driving me mental.

It's mad like, Gary is not our responsibility and yet here he is. Like a big fat seal wailing and rocking backwards and forwards on the chair. Jaysus. Daddy said 'have a bit of compassion' but I did for the last few days and enough is enough. If you don't come and get him I am going to ask Paul to arrest him for trespassing.

You have an awful cheek dumping that poor boy. What about his feelings? I think you should make up with him. Let bygones be bygones. I asked him if he would get a job and he said he would if MTV offered him a job presenting but to be honest with you he would be more suitable for wildlife programmes at the moment and I don't mean presenting them either.

I said to Daddy 'our loyalty should be with Deirdre and he has his own mother and father'. Daddy would not throw him out though. What is his mother's phone number? Do you think they might come over and get him? Have you spoken to them? What about Omar would he come over and get him even if you don't want to, it's his fault too.

Deirdre, I am getting really cross now girl, so I'd say you had better sort this out and even if you have to lie, tell Gary he can come back and you can always change your mind once he is back on English soil.

Stop ignoring me Deirdre or I will have to take serious action. And answer my questions.
Love Mammy

To: Pearse@hotmail.com
Cc: Deirdre@aol.com ; Kay@hotmail.com;
From: Mammy@ eirecom.ie
August 19th

Dear Pearse,
I am glad you are finding the current situation so
amusing. However, for me it is not funny at all.
Gary, Timmy and Daddy are out every night and
they have Mr. A with them, he's nearly an
alcoholic now I'd say. I heard them coming up the
street last night and when I looked out the window
Daddy was pushing Gary in a Dunnes Stores
trolley and Timmy had Mr. A on his shoulders.
When they got outside our gate they did the
Riverdance and by then the whole street were out.
The Hickey lads had all been out drinking too and
they brought out a load of hurleys and they were
playing hurling outside till Mrs. A's window was
smashed and she had to call the guards. It was
Paul's boss who came out and with him being
great friends with Daddy he thought it was a grand
craic altogether although thankfully he did tell
them to call it a night. He told me then they were
only lads having a laugh. Lads, I ask you, not one
of them is under 25 and some of them are much
older. I was mortified. I told him to arrest them
to teach them a lesson but I got no satisfaction.

Deirdre has washed her hands of Gary and she
said he is not her responsibility. What would you

190

think of that ? He is hardly my responsibility but I am stuck with him.

Thank you all for your presents but to be honest I have not had any time to think about my birthday this year I have far too much on my mind. I did not even go out to celebrate although we are going out tonight for a meal. All the family and Mr. and Mrs. D's and A's and Gary are coming. I hope now Gary doesn't break down in the restaurant as he breaks down at the slightest thing. If he hears a song, any song it seems to me, he starts wailing, if he sees a television programme he starts wailing, a man on the news last night reminded him of the man who lives in the flat opposite them and that started him off. If he sees a couple he starts, if he sees a couple holding hands he can become hysterical. If he sees a girl in a black dress or jeans that sets him off, the boy is a fool. No wonder Deirdre found someone else. Who could blame her.
Love Mammy

To: Deirdre@aol.com
Cc: Pearse@hotmail.com ; Kay@hotmail.com;
From: Mammy@ eirecom.ie
August 27th

Dear Deirdre
Thanks for your email. Well Gary is gone, at last.
He went out to a club with Xavier and he met a girl
from Poland and he is gone home with her, to
Poland if you don't mind. He soon got over you
then. I am delighted he is gone as he was eating
us out of house and home and costing us a
fortune in tissues. How he got a girl I don't know,
he put on about 5 stone in the time he was here
and the diet of fish suppers from the chipper gave
him pimples the size of Maltesers. Well at least if
he breaks up with the Polish girl it will be her
parents who have to put up with him. DO NOT
GIVE OMAR OUR ADDRESS OR PHONE
NUMBER.

I notice that you did not answer my questions,
do you or Omar have something to hide. The only
thing we do know now that Omar is from Egypt
and not China. Omar Sharif is from Egypt too.
There seem to be a lot of coincidences here with
regard to Omar Sharif. It had better not be him.
Too old.

Oh by the way thanks for the flowers you sent
for my birthday, they are dead now. For future
reference for you all, I don't like flowers, only in the

garden. I think flowers are a lazy present really and I would by far prefer a present of perfume, clothes, shoes, jewellery something along those lines anyway but not anything for the house as that is not a present at all. I think I have told you all this before but I may as well be talking to the wall.

I am going to my school reunion next month. I can't wait to see all my old friends, they are going to be so jealous of me. I am going to the Hayfield for all the treatments on the day. I'm not sure whether I will buy a new outfit or wear one of the outfit's I got in Italy. Although I'd say a new one may very well be on the cards. I wanted Daddy to come but it's all female and no partners are invited. I suppose it's just as well as what about the girls who never got husbands it would be embarrassing for them especially when they see the way Daddy adores me. I am looking forward to seeing the nuns as well. I was brilliant at school and the nuns loved me as did all my school friends, well most of them, the others were jealous of me.

You know I met Daddy when I was still at school. He was going out with a girl called Eileen O' Reilly. Now she was not one of the popular set and she was very plain and a bit overweight so when Daddy saw me he was instantly smitten. Eileen blamed me but it was hardly my fault that Daddy fell for me, all the boys did, what could I do. Love Mammy

To: Kay@hotmail.com
Cc: Deirdre@aol.com ; Pearse@hotmail.com
From: Mammy@ eirecom.ie
Sept 1st

Dear Kay
Happy birthday girl. I'm sorry that I have not had time yet to post your present or card but I will ring you later and sing Happy B'day to you in person. I told Daddy to post your things several times but to no avail. They are still sitting on the hall table every time I go out the door. You can blame him for you not getting the lovely skirt I bought for you from Dunnes. I got a size 14, would that be right? If not you can either go on a diet (recommended) or get a piece put into it (not recommended as that would make it size 16 and you don't want to be a size 16).

So you are 29 now, about the right age for getting married and starting a family. Yes I know you got married to Jerry, but as I have said to you many times that is in the eyes of the State of New York, and I am sure has no legal bearing anywhere else in the world although I could not swear to that; it's simple logic.

We had a great time at Daniel O' Dolan, Xavier and Julian were up on the stage dancing and Daniel O' Dolan had on a lovely jumper with a picture of the Virgin Mary on it. His mammy was not there again but I did not like to ask questions in case they had fallen out or something. Anyway

194

after the show Xavier and Julianand Daniel went out for dinner and dancing although I don't think that Daniel would be doing much dancing as he has just had a hip-replacement op. I told Xavier to ask about the mammy but he is not home yet. He was staying over at Julian's like a little sleepover but for the lads. He forgot to take his pyjamas though, I saw them above on his bed earlier and the nights are drawing in now but I suppose Julianlent him some. Deirdre did not come over to see Daniel although it would have been the ideal time for her to introduce us all to Omar but on the other hand, after the experience with Gary it is probably best for Omar not to know where we live.

It has just been brought to my attention that Mr. Michael Flatley, Lord of the Dance himself, has bought a place in Castlehyde. Now as you know, unlike some people in the family I am not a social climber. However, I do enjoy Michael's performances and so I would not mind being friends with him although I would not allow him to partake in any family holidays etc until I got to know him better. I just rang Daddy and asked him if we could take a drive down to Castlehyde to find Michael's house and pop in to see him. Daddy said no. No worries there I will get Timmy to take me later.

Nora is 5 days overdue and if she goes much longer she will burst. She is bigger than she was with either set of twins and they said this is a single baby. It must be the size of a baby hippo. That's all we are short now, a big fat ginger haired baby, it's not enough that we have 4 skinny foxies already. I'll be ashamed of my life visiting it in the hospital.

Well again, Happy B'day, did Jerry buy you anything nice? Is he a millionaire now?
Love Mammy

To: Pearse@hotmail.com
Cc: Deirdre@aol.com ; Kay@hotmail.com;
From: Mammy@ eirecom.ie
Sept 6th

Dear All

Well as you know by now the babies are here. It was twins after all. Apparently one was hiding behind the other and that's why they did not show on the scan. I'd have thought there would have been two heartbeats or some indication that there were two babies but there wasn't and no explanation was offered and Paul would not pursue it as I would have. They twins are just perfect. They have very dark hair and brown eyes. Their names are Orlaith and Aoife and they are beautiful. I love them. The only down side is that Nora's mother is sick again, back in hospital with diabetes, she is always sick that bloody woman. Especially when it comes to looking after them kids. I know that she has them every day and in the school holidays but they are her grandchildren so should I give her a medal. Anyway guess who got left holding the babies, yours truly. I am a martyr to my children. They are very bold boys all four of them. Now that Emmet and Lorcan are two they are starting to talk properly and you would not hear the language they use coming from a sailor. Ciaran and Eoin are no example to the small fellas and Timmy is no example to any of them. You'd imagine with their parents being professionals and in the Guards at that, that they would be better behaved. They love our Marie though and she plays mad games with them and then goes out and leaves me to pick up the pieces. Adam is good with them too and at least he takes them outside and plays football with them. Timmy told them to call Daniel O' Dolan a big bollix, did you ever hear the likes of that. Daniel O' Dolan is a lovely person. Then when Mrs. D came over they called her a big bollix. She was not impressed, she said to me 'I have lost a stone since May' (in her dreams like). I think that all the children should be beaten with a big stick and their mouths washed out with soap. But that is not the thing at all these days. These days it's all 'let them express themselves, let them smack you if they need to, let them steal, fight, swear, and whatever you do make sure that you support them when they become serial killers or Protestants.' It will all end in tears, mark my words.

The babies and Nora will be home from the hospital tomorrow but Daddy said the boys will have to stay here for a few days so that Paul, Nora and the babies can adjust but I think that it's to give Nora and Paul time to pack up and leave the country. No seriously though, I told Paul that he should take them all home together to avoid giving the girls a false sense of security, they should know the mayhem that they have to live in from

the start. As usual nobody listened to me and the boys will be here for a few days more. I don't mind though as Daddy is not working for a few days so he can look after them. I have my own stuff to be attending to.
Love Mammy

To: Deirdre@aol.com
Cc: Pearse@hotmail.com ; Kay@hotmail.com;
From: Mammy@ eirecom.ie
Sept 8th

Dear Deirdre

Thank you for sending the photos of Omar at last.
Very nice. His hair is lovely but I was not
impressed with his jeans at all. Dare I say they
are not well cut by any stretch of the imagination,
cheap I'd say. His shirt was nice but his shoes
could do with a good polish. You looked very nice
yourself too in the pictures and I do like your new
hairstyle.

Well, I have been very busy for the last week. I
got Timmy to take me down to Castlehyde to find
Michael Flatley's house but although we drove
around the whole place for 5 hours we could not
find it. I went into the Garda station down there
and asked them for his address but they would not
let me have it. I told them that I was considering
him as a family friend but no, they refused me
point blank. I said to Timmy 'never mind we will
come back tomorrow and search again' but Timmy
declined saying he had to go to work. I thought it
would be worth taking the day off but he did not.
He can be very disobliging you know.

Xavier saved the day though, Julian loves
Michael too and he agreed to drive around with
me the next day. I rang Paul to get the address
but he said he was too busy with the babies and

200

the boys and Nora and the dog and Nora's mother who has to stay there for a few days as the father and brothers have all gone away fishing. The mother could not go due to being in the hospital and the father and brothers were very upset as she is the only one who can put up the tents and make a camp-fire. They have to stay in a hotel now instead and Nora said that her mother had never stayed in a hotel in her life, in fact the only time she had been in a hotel was when Nora and Paul were paying. As you know Nora's father is a big farmer and I'd say he still has his Communion money. Her poor mother is exhausted from looking after him and their 10 sons. Still though it was not all bad for Nora having the 10 brothers; they are the reason she is so good as a 'hands-on' Ban Garda. She is great at tackling the rugby fans and the players when need be and any other criminals that get out of line. When there is any trouble all the lads want to partner up with Nora. She learned all her fighting skills through having to fight with the ten brothers and it's stood to her.

Paul could or would not go down to the station in Castlehyde and get the address but after several phone calls he agreed to ring and got me an email address. It's not the same as an address but I emailed Michael and asked him to email me back with his home address.

I did not get a reply within the next few hours so I came to the conclusion that Michael could be away or anything so myself and Julian decided to go down and try to find the house itself. When we got to Castlehyde I told Julian to go in the Post Office and put on an American accent and say he was Michael's son. He was to say that he had come to visit his father as a surprise but he'd lost the address and could they let them have it. Jaysus if you heard Julian's American accent he sounded Chinese and the man was onto us in a flash. He threw us out. Can you imagine me being thrown out of a country Post Office, me. I was outraged and I will be writing to the Minister for Post Offices when I get a chance. We drove around for a few hours after but to no avail, we did not find it. God alone knows where the house is. Anyway I said to Julian 'don't worry, I'm sure the address will be above when we get back'. It wasn't. He could be on tour or something so we will continue searching. I did send another email just to say that I understood he might be away but that they even had the internet in Italy so I am sure that they must have it wherever he is.

When I got up the next day my inbox was empty. Now I thought that was just pure bad manners as even if he is on tour he can't be dancing 24 hours a day and how long would it take him to email me back. I don't know why I am asking you lot as you are no great shakes at replying to emails either, I don't know why as ye were brought up with lovely manners. Anyway I sent him another email saying that I thought he would have better manners than that, him being Irish like. Still I did not want to appear to be too petulant as that would give the wrong impression entirely. I ended it by saying 'I look forward to your reply'.

It's now been 2 days and still no reply although I have sent him 29 emails so far. I will have to get Paul to get me the home address as I think now that the email address might be wrong. Paul said the address was m.Flatleylordofthedancefella@hotmail.com. That sounds about right but you never know with the internet. I am certain that he would not be ignoring me. Julian and myself will continue with the search.

Daddy is helping out grand with the boys, he took them all to McDonalds yesterday and now they are barred. Daddy is not barred but is only allowed in the drive-thru for the next six months. He doesn't mind though as he never eats anything there anyway, in fact he only ever goes with the kids or Marie. He usually gets his dinner from Timmy or the chip shop.

Love Mammy

To: Pearse@hotmail.com
Cc: Deirdre@aol.com ; Kay@hotmail.com;
From: Mammy@ eirecom.ie
Sept 10th

Dear Pearse

While I was glad to be copied on your email to your sisters, for future reference I as your mother would prefer to appear in the 'to' line of the email not the 'copy' line.

The boys are back here. They went home for a day but Eoin took Orlaith out of the cot and was just about to put her in the paddling pool with the dog when Daddy caught him so they had to come back here. The dog goes in the paddling pool to hide when they are around. The dog must have learning difficulties; going in the paddling pool makes him an easier target I should report them boys to the to the animal cruelty people. They will have to go home next week as Daddy is back at work.

Now Pearse as you did not answer me when I suggested that yourself and Mary Sullivan should get together I took it upon myself to ask her if she would be interested. She said she would definitely. I told her to email you but she said she does not have a computer so I gave her your address and you can expect a letter from her any day now, depending on the postal system in the outback of Sydney. Don't bother thanking me now, you can do that when you buy the ring! I swear she is doing great on her new medication and you can hardly notice the tic in her face at all now. She will never be a beauty I know, we can't all be beautiful, but I bet when she has had her stomach stapled she will be presentable. You can move home then and live in her house (post wedding obviously) with herself and her mother. The poor mother is bed-ridden, she has been since Mary was born 38 years ago. The only time she gets up is to go to bingo or on her holidays to Malaga.

Paul came down today and he was acting very strangely. I asked him what was the matter and he said 'do you think the girls are very dark, they have black hair, and brown eyes and olive skin and the other kids are all ginger with blue eyes and fair skin'. I said 'well they are bound to be different, the other kids are boys'. He said 'oh yeah'. He's an awful eejit that fella. At least he took the boys home at last and the house is back to normal.

Off to my school reunion tomorrow night.
Love Mammy

To: Kay@hotmail.com
Cc: Deirdre@aol.com ; Pearse@hotmail.com
From: Mammy@ eirecom.ie
Sept 14rd

Dear Kay
Thanks for your email. I am delighted that you got
your skirt and even more delighted that it was too
big. It must be the way you stand in photos. Buy
a magazine and study the way the film stars stand
in photos. Always with one leg in front of the
other, this is the best angle as it makes the hips
look slimmer.

The school reunion was an amazing success.
Almost everyone turned up except for Sadie
Murphy who is in a high security facility in
Arkansas for being a black widow. That is not the
spider with a dead husband, it just means that
she married rich men and then killed them for their
money allegedly, although I don't believe a word of
it myself. The poor girl, it is pure coincidence that
she got married eight times and each of the elderly
husbands was wealthy and that each of the
husbands died of poisoning. Sure they could have
all eaten poison by accident, they were probably
senile and she married them out of the kindness of
her heart. Now the poor girl is in prison. Even if
she had killed them what in the name of God did
they think she was marrying them for? I'm sure
that all poor young girls marry or service rich old
men for their personalities – not. I had asked the

nuns if they could do a video link-up with Sadie but they said no.

Most of the girls looked lovely but some looked dreadful, I was one of the lovely ones. Daddy's ex, Eileen O' Reilly was there which was something of a shock as I thought she lived in America but she told me she had recently been divorced and had moved back home with her 3 girls. I asked her if she was living with her sister but she said no she was buying a place of her own. According to her, her ex-husband is a wealthy property developer and they had split up as she felt that she needed to move home as she got fed up with the shallowness of life in LA. I'd say myself that she was living in a trailer. Whatever reason she is going to cost the Health Service a fortune, she is obese. She said it's from steroids she's on but I'd say it more likely from 'all you can eat' meals in America. She asked how Daddy is and I told her he could not be better. She asked for our phone number to keep in touch but I said we had no phones. I don't want her eating us out of house and home. I suppose her three girls are huge as well, all Americans are, the slim ones you see on the television have had all the fat air-brushed out.

My best friend from school, Elaine O' Mahoney was at the reunion too. She is lovely, and we are going to keep in contact now again as she only lives a couple of miles away. She is a literary agent and I asked her if she had Michael Flatley's address and she said she didn't but she thought she knew the house and drew me a map.

Some of the girls were complaining that there was no alcohol there but that would not affect me at all. The tea was grand for me. A few of us went out for a meal after and they all had wine, I had a lovely drink called Pina Colada that Xavier had told me about. I may have had it before but I'm not sure. It's lovely anyway.
Love Mammy

To: Deirdre@aol.com
Cc: Pearse@hotmail.com ; Kay@hotmail.com;
From: Mammy@ eirecom.ie
Sept 15th

Dear Deirdre

Happy birthday to you. I hope you like the Daniel
O' Dolan poster I sent, it took me ages to find it.
Does Omar like Daniel O' Dolan?

Isn't it strange that all of ye except Xavier were
born in the last four months of the year. I was a
medical miracle as I was pregnant for 11 months
with each of ye. The doctor's said that I had got
dates wrong but how could I get six wrong. I can
count. Anyway you were all big fat babies except
Xavier who was not. The reason you were all so
big was that you were all 2 months late. You,
yourself weighed 7lb. 10. Imagine that as you
know I have been slim all my life so carrying a 7lb
10 baby was an awful strain for me and I was
lucky to survive it.

Deirdre do not go to Egypt with Omar, if he
asks you, as I am worried that you might be sold
into the white slave trade or you might get
sunstroke as it is very hot out there. What did he
get you for your birthday?

I have been very busy helping Nora with the
girls. Nora's mother is better now so the boys are
down there a lot. The girls are so sweet. I have
taken them out in the pram and everyone loves

them. I bought them some lovely dresses and shoes, it's really nice shopping for girls. Boys stuff is a bit boring. When you do have kids try to have girls. Not that I don't like my boys I do they are grand for boys like. Paul's boys on the other hand are not so great but they might get better.

Nora is very down and crying a lot. I suppose it's the strain of three sets of twins. She is worn out as well and Paul is doing a lot of overtime as they can do with the extra money at the moment.

Paul drove me home yesterday and he mentioned again about the girls being dark but I pointed out to him that they are the image of Daddy and that if he had brown eyes and black hair they would be doubles of him. Daddy does get very tanned in summer. I really don't know what Paul is worried about you would think he would be thankful that they are not ginger.

I have been very lax about my health lately, I know you are all worried about it but I have been busy and as you know I always put everyone else before myself and with all the problems you lot have I don't get a moment to worry about myself. In any case I am not too keen about going to Doctor Nolan since he conspired with Daddy to cancel Xavier's holiday. Since then Daddy has refused point blank to discuss a replacement holiday for Xavier.

So I am, in effect, boycotting Doctor Nolan. I suppose the time will come when I feel sorry for him and go back to see him but it's not today for sure.
Love Mammy

To: Pearse@hotmail.com
Cc: Deirdre@aol.com ; Kay@hotmail.com;
From: Mammy@ eirecom.ie
Sept 17th

Dear Pearse
Well what can I say? I had no idea at all that Mary
Sullivan would do something like that and you
cannot seriously be blaming me. How would I
know that she would send you nude photos?
Jaysus and the size of her. I am sure that I did not
tell her that she was your girlfriend; I merely said 'it
would be grand if ye got on'. Where on earth did
she get nude photos from? Who took them, not
her mother I hope. If I were you I would send
them on to the priest and she would get a fine
shock when he came to visit her with them. You'd
think she'd have waited till after her op to have any
photos done, nude ones in particular. It will make
things a bit awkward now as I have already invited
her to dinner on Xmas day. Do you think it would
be ok for her to come as she can be very
aggressive and I do not want to invoke her temper.
If it makes you too uncomfortable though I will get
Daddy to go down there and tell her that she
cannot come. Daddy is well able to protect
himself.

I suppose a relationship with Mary is out of the
question now. However, I do know a lot of other
girls and some of them have a lot more to offer
than Mary and I am almost certain that none of

212

them would send you nude photos. Just say the word and I will have a look round for you. Do not send the photos to Timmy he would show all Cork although it might make her cop herself on. Still it's grand to see a girl that size have a bit of confidence and to be honest she will probably be a right hussy after the operation and you would not want to be putting up with anything like that in your married life. So really be grateful that you had a lucky escape. Try to be a bit more discerning about who you communicate with in the future.

It will be lovely at Xmas when you are all home and you will see the baby girls. Kay I know you will be bringing Jerry, as ye are legally married, Pearse unless we have a miracle you will be coming on your own. Deirdre will you bring Omar or would he be going to see his own family.

Let me know before the beginning of November at the latest so I can buy the Brussels sprouts. I don't want to leave it till the last minute as sprouts are like gold dust in December.

Love Mammy

To: Kay@hotmail.com
Cc: Deirdre@aol.com ; Pearse@hotmail.com
From: Mammy@ eirecom.ie
Sept 19th

Dear All
 I have some very bad news. I was wrongfully
arrested and wrongfully charged. I am contacting
Amnesty International immediately. They will be
outraged.

Julian was away for the last few weeks so we
had to put the search for Michael Flatley on hold.
He got back last Thursday and we decided to go
out again yesterday. I packed a picnic and off we
went. Now I must point out we were taking the
picnic to have in the car not to take to Michael's as
he would offer us a meal once we got there. I'd
say he is very generous like that.

So off we go but this time we were armed with
the map that Elaine had given me at the school
reunion and we had an idea where to head to.
Well X marked the spot and sure enough we found
the house. We found the front gates but it had
one of those intercom things on it and although
Julian rang and rang there was no response. We
drove around the walls and then I spotted a gap in
the bushes. I said to Julian 'let's get in that way
and give him a lovely surprise'. Julian was a bit
worried in case there were guard dogs but I told
him that I had read somewhere that Michael did

not like dogs at all, or was that Pat Kenny, who knows? One of them anyway.

The grounds were enormous and we were walking around for ages looking for any signs of human life. After about 3 hours we came to a trail that led us through trees onto a path and shortly after there was the house. I saw some French Windows and they were open, it was a lovely warm day. I said to Julian 'we may as well go in that way as the front door could be miles away'. Julian was not too sure but I headed off and he soon caught up.

We went in to the room and it was lovely but a bit dark coming in from the bright day. I said 'Michael, anyone home' and I heard a sound from the corner. We went over and there was Michael's mother sitting in an old chair. I said 'Mrs. Flatley, how's it goin'. She opened her eyes and started screaming like a banshee. It must have been the shock of seeing Julian. Well before I knew it we were surrounded by about twenty bouncer kind of fellas with batons, Garda ones. They were shouting in a language I could not understand, 'Halt, Halt'. Then another man came in and said 'who are you'? I said 'who are you and what are you doing in Michael Flatley's house, tell me immediately because my sons are policemen'. He said 'who is this Michael Flatley, this is my home, why are you here'. I thought then we had made a mistake. The man was a German businessman and he was highly irate. I tried to tell him that it was a genuine mistake but he kept on ranting and raving and of course that annoyed me a bit as it was a genuine mistake. In any case it was hardly my fault that Elaine had given me the map. I said to him 'I think you should be a bit more considerate of me after all you are a visitor in my country. My ancestors were walking on this land when yours were in Germany'. That seemed to drive him mad altogether and he told one of the bouncers to call the guards. Shur I didn't care as Paul would sort it all out but then we were taken to the Garda station in Castlehyde and arrested and charged with trespassing. Can you believe the cheek of that? I an Irish woman and Julian an Irish man trespassing for walking on Irish land. What is the world coming to?

The arresting guard was the one I had asked previously for Michael's address and I told him that it was his fault as if he had given me the address in the first place then this mistake would not have been made. He rolled his eyes to Heaven and said 'ye will appear in court next week', feckin eejit. Then I had to go home and tell Daddy and Daddy was laughing at me although he stopped laughing when I told him it was a criminal offence and that he would have to pay any fines that both Julian and I got and for the solicitors. Paul came down later on and said it would be highly unlikely that I will be sent to prison as it is a first offence. I said it is not an offence it's a simple mistake.

Either way we have to go to court now next week. The shame of it. I hope nobody finds out as it would ruin my status in the community.
Love Mammy

To: Deirdre@aol.com
Cc: Pearse@hotmail.com ; Kay@hotmail.com;
From: Mammy@ eirecom.ie
Sept 24th

Dear All

Sorry that I have not been in touch but as you know I have had a lot on my mind. We went to court this morning and thankfully the judge saw that it was a genuine mistake and not a kidnap attempt and we only got fined 10 Euro each. It was a relief but it has been an awful ordeal for both Julianand myself, so much so that we have not been to Castlehyde at all since and to be honest we might not go there again for a while.

I was very worried about ending up in prison as being as attractive as I am I would catch the attention of all the lesbian dudes and I would not have any interest in them. Although I could probably advise them on style and haircuts etc.

Some good news at last, Timmy has got the makeover that I applied for. He was a bit put out first when I told him as he was not too keen on being called 'The Worst Dressed Man in Ireland' but when I told him he had beaten thousands to get the title he said 'alright so'. He asked me if he would be lovely when he is done over and I said he would although I am afraid that that might be giving him false hope. He has to get the makeover now though as I will get a prize for introducing him. He said that as he is going on

218

television he would be watching his diet for the next few weeks. The makeover day is at the end of November. I, obviously, will accompany him. It's all first class travel and hotels so who else would go.
Love Mammy

To: Pearse@hotmail.com
Cc: Deirdre@aol.com ; Kay@hotmail.com;
From: Mammy@ eirecom.ie
Sept 25th

Dear All

I am mortified, my reputation is in tatters. I cannot believe what has happened. Daddy got the newspaper this morning and I just glanced at the headlines and they were:

FLATLEY STALKERS FINED €10.

At first I just thought that it was awful that poor Michael had to put up with stalkers and then that them being fined 10 Euros was a bloody disgrace, they should have been jailed. But I was on my way out with Mrs. D so really did not take much notice. That was until we got in the taxi and the taxi man had on the local radio and the DJ said 'you must read this article from this morning's paper, it's hysterical, in fact I will read it now for you. Two people were yesterday fined €10 each for stalking Michael Flatley. However, Mr. Flatley was never in any danger as the hapless duo stalked him to the wrong house and were arrested on being found in the home of a German businessman who wishes to remain anonymous. The businessman did comment that he was shocked to see two strangers sitting chatting to his deaf mother. He thought it was a kidnap attempt.

The judge said that he would give the defendants the benefit of the doubt that the whole thing was a mistake and said that the stalkers' names were not to be released. He also advised them to desist in their search for Mr. Flatley as next time they would not be so lucky. If anyone out there knows these two loopers ring the station now and we will give you a grand prize, we will be offering this prize for one day only so pick up the phone now, to get you in the mood here is "Riverdance"'.

What will I do if this gets out? Jaysus, surely nobody would betray me, although they betrayed Jesus himself so what hope do I have. Not too many people know and I am sure Julian would not tell anyone. I felt so bad that I had to cancel my lunch and shopping trip and go back home and lie down.

Love Mammy

To: Deirdre@aol.com
Cc: Pearse@hotmail.com ; Kay@hotmail.com;
From: Mammy@ eirecom.ie
Sept 27th

Dear All

Sorry about not emailing you but as Daddy told
you I had to get away for a couple of days to learn
how to deal with my fame. I missed Timmy's
birthday but Daddy said they had a great time at
the pub with the lads.

By the time I got home that day of the DJ
offering a prize I had already been betrayed.
Julianand I were named and shamed while I was
still sitting in the taxi. Mrs. D nearly died when she
realized it was me and came in home with me to
make me a cup of tea with a tablespoon of brandy
in it. Julian came over straight away and we
worked out between us that it had to be someone
who knew us both and who knew that we were
searching for Michael. It could not have been me
as I don't even know Julian's surname. So by the
process of elimination we worked out it was either
the guard at Castlehyde or someone who worked
in the court, or someone from within my very own
household. I was only at home an hour and
Timmy rang me and told me to put on the
television because the story was on the local
news. Then there was knocking on my door and
when I answered it was a reporter looking for an
interview and a photo. I told him no way.

222

When Daddy came home he could hardly get past the reporters outside. Apparently the story has generated great interest because it was so funny. I just went to bed for the rest of the day.

The next morning there was a headline in one of the tabloids saying that I was having an affair with Julian, that he was my toy boy. Then the same paper rang and asked if Julian and I would be interested in doing a 'tasteful' semi-nude photo. I hung up. Ten minutes later they rang again saying would I do a topless shot with Julian. Julian would be fully clothed. I was mortified and did not know what to do. Mrs. A rang me to complain that she could not get her car out of her driveway because it was blocked by reporters' cars. I told her to feck off.

Daddy came in then with the papers and the story was in every paper and the German man had done an interview saying that I had crazed eyes and that poor Julian looked like a natural born killer. What the hell is that all about? The phone kept ringing and then television cameras turned up. Then Dex Clapboard (he is a media something or other) phoned and said that he would come over to offer us some help. He did. He said that the only way to get the press off our backs was to agree to do an interview with one magazine. He advised us to go away to a secret

location in the country and he would get the best magazine deal for us and that is how we ended up doing an 8 page spread for Hiya magazine. Not only that but we also got an undisclosed sum of money and the magazine showed that I have lovely eyes and not crazed eyes. We now have interviews lined up with several shows both here and in the UK although I am not going to the UK they are coming over here to us. I don't want to be mugged. We have also been invited to GAY in London but I am not going, Julian is though.

I only got back home this morning as the magazine will be out tomorrow. I was very surprised to find that Xavier had gone to the Bahamas. I told Daddy that I was thrilled that they had made up and that he had relented and given Xavier the holiday. Daddy said he had done no such thing so I have no idea whatsoever where Xavier got the money. I bet the poor fella had to get a loan to get away from the media. Daddy said that Xavier wanted to talk to the reporters, I suppose he wanted to kill them, luckily Daddy held him back.

I am glad to be home. My publicist said that I need to be available for the press to keep the interest levels up. I suppose next all the top designer houses will be wanting me to wear their clothes.

Marie will be 19 on the tomorrow and we are having a party for her as the publicist said that 'Nearer' the magazine will pay for it. The Lord Mayor rang up and said he would love to come as did some DJ's from the local radio and the President of the Farmers Union.

Julian and I are hoping Michael Flatley will get in touch as we are too busy to go looking for him.

Someone has bought the big 6-bedroom house at the end of the close. They must be loaded as it is being refurbished from top to bottom. It will be nice to have new neighbours although I hope they won't be annoying me for autographs.

Love Mammy

To: Deirdre@aol.com
Cc: Pearse@hotmail.com ; Kay@hotmail.com;
From: Mammy@ eirecom.ie
Sept 28th

Dear Deirdre

Thanks for your email. I am glad that Omar got you a Mercedes for your birthday. He must have money so. A definite improvement on Gary.

Daddy bought Marie a little car for her birthday. I never knew she had been having driving lessons and passed her test. I am delighted that she has a car as she can take me out when Timmy and Daddy are not around. I thought I would have a chauffeur due to my newfound fame but to be honest the party was not a great magnet for celebs at all. There were a few Big Brother people there and that fat common one who used to be married to the Irish fella from that band but not Dermot O' Leary or Davina. The Lord Mayor came but left when Marie's friends started throwing the birthday cake at him. It was getting stuck in his medallion. The DJs were a disgrace and were drunk and disorderly almost from the get-go. The President of the Farmers' Union was disgusted as the catering was all veggie but as I said to him farmers produce vegetables too. The music left a lot to be desired unless you were on drugs which I think most of them were. They were all drinking champagne which seemed to make them mental. They are used to drinking cheap cider and took full advantage of the free bar.

I had bought a lovely new dress for the occasion as I did not know who might be there but to be honest it was wasted. Marie's buddies were all in jeans and when they started the food fight I had to leave as my dress would have been ruined. Daddy and Timmy stayed till the end. One of the Big Brother ones asked me if Timmy would doing any interviews in magazines or on tele and I told her he might after his makeover. She was all over him after that and he told me this morning that she said she would go on the makeover programme with him. He'd given her the wrong telephone number thank God; we would not want that type hanging around here at all.

Marie said she enjoyed it anyway and Adam and herself are off to Ibiza for two weeks tomorrow. I am doing my first television interview tomorrow. I am delighted but a little bit worried about being propelled into stardom.
Love Mammy

To: Kay@hotmail.com
Cc: Deirdre@aol.com ; Pearse@hotmail.com
From: Mammy@ eirecom.ie
Sept 29th

Dear Kay

I am in agony and was hoping you could come home to nurse me. As I wanted to look my best for my first television appearance I decided rather than shave under my arms I would put on a widely used hair removal cream. As I had tried them before and did not find them too great I thought I would let it on a bit longer than the recommended three minutes. I decided half an hour would be better. Now it *was* burning but I ignored it, beauty is pain as we well know. Well I went in the shower after and when I tried to wash it off I could not touch under my arms. I had to keep the water on and gently remove the cream with cotton wool. The pain was awful but I did not tell anyone as I thought it would be better by the morning. I had to take a bowl of water and loads of cotton wool to bed and keep putting the cold cotton wool pads under my arms. I eventually fell asleep.

When I got up the next morning I said to Daddy 'under my arms are a bit sore, I think I may have left the hair removal cream on too long'. He asked me to show him and when I lifted my arms he said 'Jaysus there are bunches of grapes under your arms look in the mirror'. I did and he was right there were blisters the size and shape of bunches

228

of grapes under my arms. Daddy said I had to go to the hospital immediately. I wanted to go on the television programme first but he would not hear of it. When we got to the hospital and I showed the triage nurse she said I would have to see the doctor immediately. The doctor was shocked and said I had severe chemical burns and would have to stay in hospital. I told him that I had to make a television appearance but he was adamant that I could not go anywhere, no way.

I told Daddy to ring Julian and let him know what was going on and he did. I had to stay in hospital for four days and I have to walk with my arms up over my head. Every time I walk past Daddy and Timmy they are saying Olè. I am thinking of suing the company. They say on the packaging leave it on for 3 minutes but they don't say do not leave it on for 30 minutes. That is surely neglect. The doctor said that in all his years as a physician he had never seen such a level of stupidity. He obviously agrees with me on the neglect issue.

To make matters worse nobody rang the television studio to say that I could not attend and would not go on his own. It's Daddy's fault because he should have phoned Dex to explain but he didn't.   Dex said we have lost the momentum as another stalker had been found up in Dublin looking for Bono. Dex said he was now representing the Dublin stalker and was no longer interested in us. He said not turning up for interviews when you were a no-letter celeb gives you a bad name in the business and that we were black-listed. He also said that he was about to put a block on my number so stop phoning him. I was livid, I told him that I was suing him for calling me a stalker, the bloody cheek of him. With his fake tan, by the time I finish with him in court he will have to make his own fake tan using tea-bags.

So there you go, it looks like I will not be going to the Oscars next year after all. At least we got an undisclosed sum of money anyway and now we can resume the search for Michael again although there is an excellent chance that he will contact me as now he knows where to find me.
Love Mammy

To: Deirdre@aol.com
Cc: Pearse@hotmail.com ; Kay@hotmail.com;
From: Mammy@ eirecom.ie
Oct 2nd

Dear Deirdre

Thank you for your email. Did I read it properly,
although I'm sure I did so that is clearly a
rhetorical question. Is Omar living with you? You
have only known him for 5 minutes so I hope that
he is not. I am almost certain that you are not a
virgin but even so you can't be living with every
man you meet. I hope to God that I have got this
wrong and he is merely your room-mate but if that
were the case where would he sleep. Xavier said
that your flat is the size of a shoebox so there is
hardly room to put another bed in there. Has he
not got a flat of his own to live in. If he is rich
surely he has his own place. What is his address?
Let me know the living arrangements immediately.

Things are grand here except for Paul's
constant comments with regard to the babies. It
was wearing Nora out and there is a tension in
their house that was never there previously. He
kept saying that he just cannot understand why
they are so dark and people are making remarks
about their colouring. I had to sit him down and
tell him a family "truth". I said to him 'now as you
know I never talk about my family too many
skeletons in too many closets and that's why the

loss of fame did not bother me so much. Well Paul, yes the girls are dark-skinned and they do have brown eyes and dark hair but there is nothing unusual about that, my own great-grandmother was Black. (I am not lying about that; her name was Betty Black). I said it is showing through now genetically, that's all. It does not matter what anyone says about the girls, they are our little babies and we have to mind them and love them no matter what. He was amazed that my great-grandmother was black although I don't know why as loads of people are called Black. He seemed to be better after that and if he had made any assumptions, then that was a mix-up on his part, I would not mislead anyone. The important thing here is the babies so Paul and Nora need to pull it together not just for the babies but for the boys and for themselves too. For all I know Nora's family may be black somewhere down the line but I am not going to be doing a family-tree investigation any time soon. Now this is top secret and not to be discussed with anyone else outside of or within the family.

After much soul-searching myself and Julian have decided to put off the search for Michael Flatley until after Xmas. Xmas is a very busy time for everyone and although I was looking forward to spending New Years Eve at Michaels there is nothing to be done.

I have just had a phone call with very bad news. Mrs D is going to America for at least 6

months. Tina is pregnant and things are not going as well as they could be and she wants her mother over there with her. I understand that Tina needs her mother but I need her too. She is my best friend and has been since we were ten years old and I depend on her to always be there when I need her as I am here when she needs me. Mrs D is leaving next week, she said she probably will come home a couple of times in between (Tina is only 9 weeks gone now) now and when the baby is born but I don't know if she will or not. I am so upset I know we can phone and email and things but it's hardly the same and I know that; I live like that with you three already and it is not ideal. Still, I would do exactly the same thing if any one of you needed me so I can only wish her luck and hope that she won't be too lonely and miss her hubby and family and friends and me too much. I will miss her though and to make matters worse I have had a pain in my head for the past week, it must be all the stress.
Love Mammy

To: Deirdre@aol.com
Cc: Pearse@hotmail.com ; Kay@hotmail.com;
From: Mammy@ eirecom.ie
Oct 4th

Dear Deirdre

I am delighted that both you and Omar are coming home for Xmas. Now are you sure Omar's mother would not prefer him to go home to her house to celebrate. I don't mind if he goes to his mother's at all really. Pearse and Kay and Jerry are coming as well. Omar can share Xavier's bedroom. He was highly insulted last year when Gary refused to share with him and although I had never liked Gary much, that made me very cross. But I am sure I will have no reason to dislike Omar and am certain that he will not do anything to make me cross.

Paul had a lovely birthday yesterday. We all went out with for a Chinese meal. It went very well considering the twins were trying Kung Fu moves on the waiters as they were serving people's meals. The Chinese people know Paul and Nora through being in the guards so they were nice enough about it.

By the way we had an email (yes they have the internet in the former USSR now too) from Gary and he is not too happy at all in Poland. The Polish girl dumped him and he is now living with her parents on a farm in the middle of Poland. God help them. It's very cold there and his television presenting career has ground to a halt. The main problem with the career is that they have loads of good-looking Polish presenters who can actually speak Polish. Gary, on the other hand is around 28 stone, balding, with a bad case of adult acne. Does the boy not have a mirror? Anyway he wanted to know if he could come over for Xmas. He said to tell you that the Polish girl was a mistake and he was clearly on the re-bound. He also asked me to ask you if he can have his collection of bus tickets back. Apparently he has kept every bus ticket he has ever bought. Why? I asked him if he had kept all the tube tickets too but he said no, you would have to me an awful eejit altogether to collect tube tickets. Hmm.

I wrote back to him and told him that I would think you would have mistaken the bus tickets for rubbish and thrown them out by now. I told him that he cannot come for Xmas as we are moving house. I said to try to make things work with the Polish girl as you were getting married and I said the best career advice I could give him was to become a bus conductor on the Polish buses and then he could have all the tickets he likes.

He wrote back asking if Daddy would lend him the money for a plane ticket back to Cork, Cork if you don't mind. Why would he want to come back here. If he had asked for a ticket to London I would have sent the money but he is not coming back here. I told him that we had no money, although we have, and I said that unfortunately when he made the decision to go to Poland with the Polish girl that he had opted out of our family and there was no way back in. Shur I was delighted that he went to Poland but he doesn't need to know that.

You still have not informed me of Omar's living arrangements and Daddy is demanding to know. It's none of my business but Daddy is nearly demented with worry. Be a good girl now and email me back straight away to put your Daddy's mind at rest.

I am going for an eye test this week as I think I must need new glasses as the pain in my head seems worse when I'm watching tele. I used to have something similar when I was younger but once I got my glasses it was fine so I suppose I need a new prescription. I have not been for about five years
Love Mammy

To: Pearse@hotmail.com
Cc: Deirdre@aol.com ; Kay@hotmail.com;
From: Mammy@ eirecom.ie
Oct 5th

Dear Pearse

I am looking forward to seeing you, not too long to
go until I Christmas and you will be home safely.
It'd be lovely now if you meet a nice girl here and
join the guards. You'd get a lovely uniform free
and pyjamas with the Garda badge. And maybe a
gun, you'd never know. Due to my recent flurry of
activities I have not had any time to look for a girl
for you but there is good news that may help in
your search for a wife.

Yes, Timmy had his makeover and he is
handsome. I could not believe it was him when I
saw him. He has got a new hairstyle, clean teeth,
and a new suit. He had lost weight and I swear he
looks completely different. He won the whole
series and he is doing a modelling spread for
some magazine or other. I said to him 'make sure
you keep yourself clean till then'. I am delighted
for him, he is not bad looking at all underneath
although he was an ugly child. I remember going
to see him when he was born and saying to Mary-
Anne 'is there something wrong with him, his
forehead is huge, did you have an affair with
Frankenstein?' Allegedly there was nothing wrong

with him but Mary-Anne did get terrible post-natal depression.

I was a bit disappointed with my prize for introducing Timmy into the competition. The prize was a basket of beauty products, and I have more beauty products than Brown Thomas. I'll give it to Mary-Anne for Xmas.

So the good news is that if Timmy does keep himself clean you, him, Xavier and Julian can all go out and get girlfriends for yourselves. I hope Deirdre learned her lesson last year and will keep Omar well away from Timmy.

With regard to my Xmas presents, don't worry boy. I don't want anything as I have everything except a pink diamond ring which I am expecting from Daddy. Still you are very organized buying your presents already. Spend your money on Xavier, as you know he is on the dole and don't bother about me or Daddy.
Love Mammy

To: Deirdre@aol.com
Cc: Pearse@hotmail.com ; Kay@hotmail.com;
From: Mammy@ eirecom.ie

Oct 6th

Dear Children

I know I have written already today but I am just telling you how bad I feel.

Mrs D is gone, my best friend is gone. I am distraught. I was so upset at the airport that I somehow lost my balance and fell down, everyone was looking at me. I was so embarrassed and to make matters worse Daddy was laughing and telling the people watching that I'd had one too many when I did not even have a drink. Daddy is not as funny as he thinks he is at all.

I am really cross with Daddy and hope one of you will mention it to him as I'm not speaking to him.

Love Mammy

To: Deirdre@aol.com
Cc: Pearse@hotmail.com ; Kay@hotmail.com;
From: Mammy@ eirecom.ie
Oct 7th

Dear Deirdre

Excuse me now my dear, I thought that Daddy was nearly demented worrying about your living arrangements, what caring father wouldn't be? I must have misheard him. It was not very nice of you to ask Daddy though, as it makes me look like a liar when I clearly made a mistake.

No, I will not be cooking anything different this year. My Xmas dinner is the best in the world and it is so special that when I offered to make it one Easter Daddy said 'no, don't that would only spoil it for Xmas girl'. As you know I don't cook that often because I don't have a lot of spare time with all my various good works etc but I always do the Xmas dinner regardless of how tired it makes me.

Xavier is not himself at all. He had a very mixed re-action to Timmy's makeover. He liked the new look certainly but he felt that Timmy had no right to be doing a modelling spread as being a model is one of Xavier's future plans and everyone knows that. He asked Timmy if he could do the modelling instead but Timmy said that he did not think that would be allowed as it was the winner of the competition that the magazine wanted. Xavier then turned on me and said why had I not put him in the competition; he would have won it hands

240

down. I tried to explain that he did not need a makeover that he was perfect and you cannot improve on perfection. He was still very cross and said I was to line up some go-sees with modelling agencies for him if I did not want to ruin his life. Of course I don't want to ruin his life so I have phoned around all the modelling agencies in Cork and made appointments for him. I expect he will be a super model before Xmas. I don't really know why he did not look into the modelling thing before but I suppose he has so many options open to him that he did not want to opt for one without researching the others. Shur it must be difficult having so many talents and so many paths to choose from. Not that he would not be successful in any career he chooses he would. The thing is by choosing one he is letting all the others down so obviously he needs to be in a career where the most people can benefit from his benevolence. Super modelling would be great as then everyone in the world will get a chance to see him.

I went for an eye test this morning and after the first simple tests he started looking at my eyes through the machine. He stopped and said 'there appears to be something there that your doctor would need to look at.
Make an appointment with your doctor and I will send him a letter. When you see him he will advise you about coming back for glasses'.
Love Mammy

To: All
From: Mammy@ eirecom.ie
Oct 9th

Dear All
I went to the doctor this morning and he did some tests using a tuning fork and reflex hammer and examined me with an ophthalmoscope. Then he sent me to the out-patients clinic for blood tests and X-rays. I have to go back tomorrow for the results. At the moment I don't know what if anything is wrong so don't be worried.
Love Mammy

To: Mrs D@gmail.com
From: Mammy@ eirecom.ie
October 9th

Dear Noreen

Thanks very much for your email. Glad all is going
well in New York and that Tina is feeling better.
Having her Mammy with her will make all the
difference. We were very lucky as we were
pregnant together with our first and second,
otherwise I would have been lost. I didn't know
anything about having babies and neither did you,
Remember when the doctor wanted to do an
internal on you and you said only Mr D was
allowed any access in that area. The doctor must
have thought we were simple. They told me my
due date was 31st of May and that day I got up
early had my hair done , did my nails, put on my
best smock, did my make-up and put my bag by
the front door. I wanted to look my best when the
baby saw me and I wanted the hospital staff to
think 'look how composed and lovely she looks'.
What an eejit. The baby finally came on June 10th
and by then I was so fed up of waiting I hardly
brushed my teeth and I was so huge that I went to
the hospital in Daddy's army pyjamas. Still Xavier
was worth the wait (most of the time anyway). We
were very innocent in those days though.

Noreen I have to tell you something that I am a
bit worried about but keep it to yourself as I don't
want the kids knowing too much and you know my

Kay and your Tina hardly go a day without contact. I went to get an eye test a couple of days ago and since then have been having all sorts of tests. They asked me if I had been having any trouble with my balance and I said no although I did fall down at the airport and I have misjudged the steps a couple of times but managed to save myself from falling hard. I did not say but I did find myself at the bottom of the stairs a couple of weeks ago. I was face down and got terrible bruising on my arm and leg and the side of my head was killing me. I had had a few drinks but I have drank a lot more before and never passed out which is what I assumed I had done. I told everyone I had slipped on the path when I was washing it down. Hubby did not say a word but he knows I never wash down the path why would I when I have a fine healthy husband. Why have a dog and bark yourself!   Anyway I asked the nurse what the tests were for and she said they can be used for all sorts of diagnoses, she named a few but I only heard brain tumour. I am praying it is not. I am so worried though, say a prayer for me that it is not a tumour please Noreen.

I miss you such a lot. I'm glad I can tell you I miss you as I never say anything like that to the kids it would upset them and make them feel guilty and they should not feel guilty as they are only doing the things all grown-up children do. It's best not to mention emotional stuff to them as it avoids upset.

I will let you know how the tests turn out tomorrow. I could be worrying us over nothing and knowing me I probably am.

Love Áine

To: Deirdre@aol.com
Cc: Pearse@hotmail.com ; Kay@hotmail.com;
From: Mammy@ eirecom.ie
Oct 10th

Dear Deirdre, Kay and Pearse
I went back to the doctor this morning and I have
to go for another test just to make sure that there
is nothing wrong.
Don't feel you have to rush home although Tina
came home when her mother was in hospital. But
money is no object for Tina as I would imagine it's
not with you Kay. But still don't waste money
flying home to be with your mother, as there is
probably nothing wrong and you could use that
money to buy your own place in the Hamptons.
Likewise you Deirdre, not that you have any
money anyway with you having had to support
Gary for all that time. Pearse don't dream of
coming all the way from Australia, you are needed
there to uphold the law and keep the peace, you
know what those Aussies are like. As I said
anyway there is probably nothing wrong but if
there were I would have no regrets except that we
did not go on one last holiday to West Cork as I
wanted to last year, remember. Or maybe I do
have other regrets. Thinking back on my life now,
should I, instead of having children, have pursued
a career with all the talents that I have. I did have
a job once in Customers Complaints but was

asked to leave before lunch as there were too many customers' complaints about me. The customers were all jealous of my appearance. I have had to deal with jealousy for most of my life. People were jealous of me of course, I was never jealous of anyone.

So don't worry about me I was born alone (except for me mother and the hospital staff) and if I have to I will suffer alone, (except for Daddy and the medical team) if indeed there is suffering to be done.

Love Mammy

To: Mrs D@gmail.com
From: Mammy@ eirecom.ie
October 14th

Dear Noreen

Thanks very much for your email. It did cheer me up before we went to the doctor, although I don't really think that I could justify leaving the family to spend Xmas and New Year in New York, especially with Pearse, Kay and Deirdre travelling home to spend the holidays with me. Now Noreen don't get me wrong, I'd love to come over to see you but as you know girl I'd never leave my family for Xmas. In any case I know you too well and I know you only suggested it to take my mind off the other. We went back to the doctor this morning and they are sending me for a MRI after the weekend. We won't know the results until after the following weekend as the radiologist has to interpret it and then let the doctor know. I am not going to think about it now again until I go for the results. I have told the kids I am going for another test but I put a positive spin on it as I really don't want them to worry. I am being the same as I always am with them, the woman who gets on with life and has accepted the fact that half her family live away from home. I do often hint that I would be happier if they were here but as I have told you many times I would never say how sad and lonely it makes me feel as they have every right to live

248

where they like and making them feel guilty about their choices would only make them resent me so I write in a way that makes them think I am having a great time regardless of where my kids are. I suppose it does get easier as time goes on, or at least you learn to live with it. You know that yourself with two of yours living away now. I thought that the emails I was sending them were funny and informative. That is what I thought until you told me that Tina told you that some of my emails were very upsetting for the girls and even Pearse was upset by some of them.

I started sending the emails when they were at uni and I thought they would end when they graduated. When I found out that Kay was going to America to work I could not believe it. I knew she was planning on going to the US but I thought it was only for a couple of months to hang out with some of the friends she had made at Med School. I was devastated when she told me that she had been offered and accepted a job there. She said she did not tell me what she was planning in case it had not worked out and she did not get the job. She knew I would worry in case she got the job because then she would leave home or in case she did not get the job as I would worry about why she was not good enough. We had a terrible argument that night. Kay said most graduates only had to worry about whether or not they would get jobs while she had to take my feelings about any decision she might make into consideration . She said my feelings were her first consideration when she chose which Med School she went to. She wanted to go to Med School in either the US or the UK but I got so 'sick' with depression that she felt she had to study in Ireland. She said that it had been the same all through her childhood whatever she wanted to do was always over-ruled by what I wanted her to do. She wanted to join the Girl Guides while I wanted her to do ballet and as they both met on Thursday evening she had no choice, I had enrolled her in ballet which she hated.   She said that Daddy always had to appear to agree with me or I would make his life miserable. She told me that Daddy had allowed her to give up ballet after the first term when he told me that the teacher had told him that we were wasting our money as she could not dance. She did then get to join Guides and stayed in it for years, until she went to Med school in fact. I told her working in a hospital in America would not be like Scrubs if that was what she thought, she just looked at me and said 'Mammy you are impossible you are supposed to be the parent supporting your children and putting your children first not trying to make us feel guilty when we decide anything that goes against what you want. We are all fed up with you manipulating us so in future just butt out.'

The rest of the children were in the room and not one of them said a word to defend me so I gathered from that that they all felt the same and I decided that from then on I would not interfere with their lives. It has not worked out like that really, I do give them bits of advice here and there but always making sure that they know it is only my opinion and no pressure is being put on them to agree with me. But it is hard not to interfere when you see them making huge mistakes, like Deirdre with Gary, anyone could tell that he was never going to make anything of himself and that it would always be Deirdre who would have to take responsibility for everything. I know he was a nice enough fella but he was not what I wanted for her at all. I think she should have somebody she can rely on now and then when times get tough. I suppose it's old fashioned of me but while I agree with equality in relationships I do believe that the man should be that bit stronger and be a bit more supportive especially with money and with doing the gardening. I mean if the woman is in the lead financially then what would she need a man for at all?

So what I am trying to say is that over time I have tried to 'butt out' but when I read over some of the emails that I have sent I think that instead of being less interfering I look to be more critical and very controlling. Telling Kay when to have children and what religion they should be, that is awful and worse still I appear to be jealous of her social life when I am in fact delighted that she has done so well for herself. Then telling her she was putting on weight. I thought she was and I thought that mentioning it would encourage her to take some action to correct it. I know what it is like to put on weight and not even realise that you are doing so. Remember when I put on all that weight when the kids were young; it was awful. Getting it off again was really difficult. I did not go out socially for months because every time I got ready to go out I would try on loads of outfits but each one of them would look worse than the one before. I lost all my confidence and would end up crying and not going out. To make matters worse I took it out on everyone around me especially hubby. Martial relations came to a complete standstill because I hated myself so much. It was awful and that is the reason that I mentioned that Kay was putting on a bit of weight. I wanted her to lose the few pounds she had put on so that she would not have to go through the same things that I had but reading back it looks like I was berating her. If I had explained my experiences my comments would not have seemed so harsh.

Looking back on the emails from this year they are not at all like what I thought they were. I thought they were all light and upbeat but some of them were very critical and I'd go so far as to say that some of them were cutting. I wanted the emails to be a running commentary on what was happening with the rest of the family and while some of them are just that, others are not too nice at all. One of the main themes seem to be about how great I think Xavier is at the expense of everyone else. I'm not at all happy about them Noreen and will spend the next few days trying to mend some of the damage. I wanted to be a modern, supportive mother but instead I am coming across as selfish and only caring about Xavier. I know I don't have much experience of mothering having grown up in the Home myself but clearly I am letting my sadness at their being away from home look like bitterness.

Noreen I do want to thank you for telling me about the emails as now that I know what is going on I really want to speak to the girls and Pearse about it. The thing is I cannot just say 'I have noticed that my emails might not be saying what I want them to say' they know I am not a reflective sort of person' so the only thing I can do is to say that you mentioned it which means that will also put Tina in the picture and I don't want to cause problems for you with your girl but in case anything comes of these medical tests I want to try to make things right with them. I would like to do that before the test results are back because if they are bad then it could seem that is the reason I want to make amends. Would you ask Tina if I can say how I found out that they were unhappy, I'd say you will have to tell Tina about the tests but that is okay as long as she only knows what my kids know.

Can you let me know asap please, I have a lot of making up to do.

Noreen I was just thinking if things were normal and you were here we would be going to see Daniel O' Dolan tonight. Xavier wanted me to go but it just would not be the same. If things go well and he plays in New York I will come over there to see him with you.

Love and miss you girl

Áine.

To: Mrs D@gmail.com
From: Mammy@ eirecom.ie
October 18th

Hello again Noreen
Thanks for phoning last night. Tell Tina thanks too but I was thinking about it and decided I would just email the children saying 'it has been brought to my attention' although that seems very aloof; I will say 'I heard that…. As far as we know they might have discussed it all with Daddy and/or other members of the family. By doing it that way I won't get anybody into trouble.

Noreen I am worn out I had Paul's kids here all day and they are a bit wild to put it mildly. I was sitting with them having a snack and looking around at each of them I got very sad. I could not help thinking if I have a brain tumour and the prognosis was bad I will not be around to see them grow up, I know I have not spent as much time with them as I should have but then I thought I had all the time in the world to spend. I know they can be terrors but they are also really funny and very affectionate and so beautiful regardless of the foxy hair. I was listening to them talking to each other and they are such great friends with each other and not just siblings. I asked each of them what they wanted to be when they grow up and they wanted to be footballers or join the police but Eoin wants to be a rapper so he can have a gun. Apparently they all have them on tv. Sitting

255

there watching them and listening to them made me think I should spend a lot more time with them and I will from now on.

The Hickey boys took them out after lunch to play football and now they are all gone for a walk out the country.

I have not said anything to the kids yet about my emails upsetting them.   I will do it tomorrow when I have had more time to think about what I want to say, hopefully . For now I am just emailing them as normal.

Love Áine

To: Pearse@hotmail.com
Cc: Deirdre@aol.com ; Kay@hotmail.com;
From: Mammy@ eirecom.ie
Oct 20th

Dear All

Are you all packed for coming home? Are Jerry
and Omar packed, although Deirdre I suppose
how would you know about Omar's packing if he
has his own flat, does he? I don't think you should
be serious with him just yet now, take your time. I
can't believe you are bringing him home already
although it will be nice to meet him I'm sure.

I went and bought the sprouts this morning .
You can keep them in the fridge for weeks safely
and I did not want to take the chance of not being
able to get any come Christmas week. You
cannot have Christmas dinner without sprouts.
That was a joke by the way, I will prepare and
freeze the sprouts of course, we don't want to
poison our guests.

I don't know what to get Jerry for Xmas, I might
get him a nice poster of Barbara Streisand, I
believe she is Jewish also. I bet Jerry buys quality
presents, he has loads of money but still your poor
sister wants to go out to work instead of having a
lovely life like Tina, shopping, gym, beauty
treatments etc. And God knows your sister could
do with it more than Tina. I may have to have a
private word with Jerry over Xmas.

Xavier and myself are in shock. The dole have said that he has to work as a postman over Christmas or his money will be stopped. Xavier a postman! I knew something was wrong when he went to sign on and the boy who worked at the dole phoned saying Xavier was having a panic attack and someone had to get him. Timmy went down to get him but when they came in Xavier was hardly able to breathe never mind speak. I gave him a brown paper bag to breath in and read the note that the boy in the dole had given him explaining about the job. The poor child has to work 6 days a week from 15th Dec up to and including the 24th Dec. Christmas Eve, that is inhumane. He has to start well before the dawn and won't finish till midday. And he will have to wear a jacket that is not custom made for him; rather it belonged to someone else. That boy has never even worn a handed down sock. I immediately rang Dr Nolan and he said that if Xavier wanted to come down in the evening he could but that getting a job for 8 days was not a medical emergency and he would certainly not be making a house call. I then rang Daddy's solicitor who was in court. I told the secretary to ring his emergency number and get him out of court. He would have known what Xavier's rights are. She said no that I did not understand he was up in court himself for fraud and that he might not be able to ring back for a long time. She let me speak to one of the others though and it took him 35 minutes at €5 a minute to tell me that it was not against the law for Xavier to have to work without him applying for a job, even if it was Xmas. So it looks like he will have to do it. Daddy said it will give him a bit of practice for when he gets a full-time job but you can't just expect someone to drop all their Xmas plans to deliver the post.

This will ruin Xavier's Christmas. He has plans to go out every night and normally he doesn't get home till morning. Daddy was no help he said Xavier can pick up the post and deliver it all on his way home. I did ask Daddy if he would do the delivering but he said no, he had his own job.

Xavier has been upstairs crying since. He only stops crying to ring down for food and drink on his mobile. It's awful.

I had to look after the boys today when the babies went for some baby thing As soon as they got here they were knocking on Xavier's door singing 'Postman Pat' , they are very bold boys. By 12 o' clock I could stand it no longer and I asked the teenage Hickey boys to take them out for a while. Two hours later there was a banging on the door and when I opened the door Eoin and Ciaran were standing on the drive with a horse. Yes, a horse. They were smiling up at me and said 'we found a horse can we bring him in'? I was stunned or beyond stunned. I said where did ye find it and Ciaran said 'in a field out-long, the big boys opened the gate to get him out and they said we can keep him, can he come in nana'? I said 'don't call me nana, call me Bibi like I told ye' (Bibi is Indian for Nana, I think.)   Then I said 'you can't bring the horse in I just washed the floor, tie him up out there until your Daddy gets back '. I had no idea what to do with a horse. They were not happy but the horse was not coming in. The house is full enough with Timmy.

They stayed outside with the horse and within minutes every child in the neighbourhood was outside feeding the horse apples, carrots, sweets and anything else they could find. But then the guards turned up. Someone had to have phoned them. They said that the horse had been stolen from a field out near Murphy's rock and that the farmer wanted to press charges, however, Paul and Nora and the babies turned up just then so another calamity was avoided as Paul knew the guards. The boys were hysterical when the horse was taken away and now they want nothing else but a horse for Christmas. I was glad when they all went home although I did go down and tell them Hickey boys that they should not have been giving horses that don't belong to them to children.

It won't be long now till ye are all here. Poor Xavier will be worn out from being a postman by then.
Love Mammy

To: Deirdre@aol.com
Cc: Pearse@hotmail.com ; Kay@hotmail.com;
From: Mammy@ eirecom.ie
Oct 22nd

Dear All

Oh Jaysus I am in total shock. You will never believe who is moving in down the road. It's Daddy's ex Eileen O' Donavan and her American daughters. I am outraged. How dare she.

I went down to welcome the new neighbours and she opened the door. She pretended she was shocked to see me but I think she knew very well where we lived and she has moved in to be close to Daddy. Then she asked me where our house was and I told her, and she said that she thought gypsies lived in there as there was usually a horse tied up outside. What a bloody liar. That horse was there once.

I went home and phoned Daddy but he didn't know anything about it and he assured me that he had no interest in any woman only myself.

Realistically I can see that no man would prefer Eileen O' Donavan over me. I am lovely and have kept my figure but I don't want her moving in here asking Daddy to change the light bulb or cut the grass or any general handyman stuff. Not that if she did she would be sadly disappointed, Daddy could not put a nail in the wall without knocking the wall down and I have to get a man to cut the grass after Daddy cut through the cord and nearly killed himself. But still. I have told Daddy that he is to drive out the other way in future and not in front of her house. I am thinking of moving the family away to a far nicer area I did say that we will need a bigger place anyway now that Timmy is a permanent feature. But obviously I won't be moving before Xmas.

Xavier said she is a fat blob anyway, Trailer Park Trash, without the trailer. Then Timmy came in and said 'who are the babes moving in down the road?' It seems the daughters are not taking after their mother.

Timmy said he was going down to welcome them but I told him to stay in as he could hardly welcome them when he was only a lodger here. He needs to know which side his bread is buttered on.

By the way I am appalled at your lack of concern regarding Xavier's ruined Xmas. In fact Pearse, I thought that I detected a note of mockery in your email. Jealousy is not an attractive feature in anyone
Love Mammy

To: Mrs D@gmail.com
From: Mammy@ eirecom.ie
Oct 30th

Dear Noreen
I don't really know how to say this but I went for
my results this morning and I have a brain tumour.
It looks to be Grade 1 or 2 but the doctor said they
really won't know until they do a biopsy.
Apparently Grade 1 has the best prognosis. He
asked me if I had any questions and I said no
although I do. I have millions. My poor husband
just broke down, I have never seen him so upset.
I am strangely calm.
    When we got home John said that we have to
tell the kids. I'm not too sure we should say
anything until after the biopsy. After all a biopsy is
another test. I know from the leaflets the doctor
gave me that I will be in hospital for a few days
and of course we will have to tell them that. I want
to say to the kids that I am going in for more tests
and leave it at that but John thinks that they have
a right to know the truth. I'll have to think about it.
Noreen I am amazed at how calm I am.
Love Áine

To: Mrs D@gmail.com
From: Mammy@ eirecom.ie
Oct 30th

Noreen

I'm not calm now. It has just hit me what this could mean. I could die. I know we will all die one day in the future but a brain tumour means the future is now for me. I could be dead in a few weeks. I do not want to have a biopsy, it will be painful and they will shave my head or part of it and I like my hair as it is.

John has hardly stopped crying since we found out. I don't know what to say to him. I said I was sorry and that made him cry louder as he said it was not my fault. In between sobs he keeps saying 'tell the kids'. I said 'perhaps you could stop crying and tell them or email them as they can all read their emails on their phones'. I only said that so he would stop crying. Marie walked in and saw him crying and said 'give him the divorce Mammy for God's sake'. He said 'Marie we have to..........and I cut him off and said 'Marie we have to go out as one of Daddy's friends is not well.' That seemed to send him over the edge as he fell on his knees and said 'oh the bravery'. Marie threw her eyes up to Heaven and went back upstairs with her snacks. I said then 'This has to stop love, I know it's a shock to you but we have to handle it better than this. Let's go down to the pub now and make a plan about how we can deal with this. I had to get him out of the house as Marie and her friends were in her bedroom and Xavier and Timmy were watching tv down the hall. I definitely do not want the children to find out like this, with their Daddy hysterical.

We did go down to the pub but really it did nothing to take our minds off it. It's too big.

John is supposed to be strong for all of us and usually he is, always there in any situation, getting me out of the little predicaments I might find myself in and saving the kids from all sorts of troubles. I don't know what to do with him being like this. I really need somebody to talk to and I suppose John does to. I mean somebody who knows about this sort of thing. I will speak to the doctor tomorrow and see what advice he can give me.

Noreen I am so scared. I want to grow old with John and I want to see my grandchildren grow up and most of them have not even been born yet. John is asleep now, he is exhausted God love him, worn out. It is years since I have looked at him asleep and I had forgotten how innocent he looks and how long I used to spend just watching him sleep. That was before the kids of course and I suppose that in the back of my mind I always thought that all that stuff would come back again once the children were all settled. So I have made myself a little promise, I will whenever I get the chance spend a bit of time looking at John sleeping so I can take the memory with me wherever I have to go.

Noreen I know how hard this is for you too but before John you were the nearest thing to family I had so I need you to be strong for me girl.
Love Áine

To: Mrs D@gmail.com
From: Mammy@ eirecom.ie
Nov 2nd

Dear Noreen
Thanks for your email. Of course you cannot
come home. Noreen think of Tina here now.
Remember what it was like when you were first
pregnant, it is scary. We had each other to go
through it all and Tina needs you now as we
needed each other. She is in a strange country
and as you said yourself his family have a
tendency to take over, with them being Italian. No
you must stay with Tina. If things change after the
biopsy I will tell you. You are my only sister, if not
by blood, by everything else and I will tell you if I
need you to be here. At this moment I want you to
stay with Tina.
    We went to the doctor this morning. John was
a little better after his sleep, I did not really sleep
much, I had several mugs of hot chocolate but it
did not make me sleepy. At least it gave me time
to write down some questions that I wanted to ask
the doctor. I have decided that I don't really want
to know too much about the medical side of it all. I
have been reading about it all on the internet and
the more I read the more confused I am. A lot of
the treatment is tailored towards the individual
these days so no two people will have the same
treatment and most of the stuff on the internet may
not even apply to me and I think that the less that I

267

know the better. It is scary reading about all the different types of tumours and what can go wrong. I think for me it is enough to know I am being treated and I will let the medical team deal with the medical stuff and do what they tell us at each stage. Of course being me I will make sure that I am having the best treatment and once we tell Kay I will ask her to keep an eye on things and she will probably know somebody on the team here as she works on the brain too. So the questions I asked the doctor were mainly where we could speak to somebody who had gone through this themselves. The doctor gave us a list of charities and support groups. He also said that he was glad that we did not want to discuss the medical issues as he himself has only a general idea and that it would be best to discuss those things with the consultant who we are going to see next week. He did say that Grade 1 and 2 tumours are considered benign because they are usually very slow growing and often surgery alone can be an effective treatment for this type of tumour. Of course he said all tumours are different and even Grade 1 and 2 tumours can be life-threatening if located in a vital area. So you see what I mean Noreen even something as simple as the grading of the tumour can be a minefield and there really is no point in worrying about it until we have an idea of what we are actually dealing with. So I have made myself another promise, I am going to try to think about the tumour as little as I possibly can as obsessing over it will not help. I am quite good at ignoring things that I don't want to think about so hopefully it will work, at least a little, with this too. Usually I am ignoring things like my jeans are a bit tight or I need to keep an eye on what I am spending, they are easy enough to ignore though.

Before we left John asked him if he thought we should tell the kids and he said that while it is clearly a personal matter if it were him with the tumour he would tell everyone who needed to know. I said to him 'if you were the person who was going to be told one of your parents had a tumour would you like to know as soon as they were told or would you like to carry on with your normal life for just a little while longer?' He said 'Well I've not heard it put like that before.' I said 'You know we keep surprises secret for as long as we can, even though that is good news we are giving to each other but we are in such a rush to tell bad news, I think it should be the other way round, keep the bad news to yourself as long as is possible and give the good immediately.' The doctor said 'I have been your doctor for so long now that I don't care to remember and as usual you will make your own mind up and damn the consequences'. As we were leaving he said 'John I'm going to prescribe you something to help you calm down, take it if you need it, it would be better if you don't but under the circumstances I think you should have it there as your wife really has enough to deal with now and she needs you to be strong for her, come back and see me again in a couple of days. Things will have changed a lot by then I'd say. It's the shock you see that's what it is now but that will change.'

John does not believe in taking tablets at all as you know but I made him get the prescription and as he broke down again as soon as we got in the door I then made him take the tablets and thankfully they knocked him out and he has been asleep in bed for hours which is giving me the chance to think over whether or not to tell the kids, I know I have to tell them something but how much is what is concerning me.

Love Áine

To: Mrs D@gmail.com
From: Mammy@ eirecom.ie
Nov 5th

Dear Noreen

It was lovely to speak to you last night, thanks for ringing I really needed to just talk to you and it was nice to laugh and forget about that oul thing in my head for a few minutes at least.

John had work this morning and I made him go. He did not want to go but I said to him I need some sense of normality and you going would make me feel better. He said he was not going. Then Marie saved the day. She came down stairs at what is an ungodly hour for her , dressed and kitted out with iPod, phone, iPad, DVD player with DVDs (for Daddy) fleecy blanket, small pillow, make-up kit, nail kit, travel wash bag, magazines and snacks. 'Daddy get ready, remember we are spending the day in Dublin once you have dropped off the work stuff, you haven't forgotten have you, you said we could stay overnight if I wanted but I have not brought enough stuff to do that although we can always buy the stuff up there if we need to. We will have a look and see who's playing up there tonight and then decide, I am so excited we are meeting some pals for lunch'.

Her phone rang and off she went. I said to John 'see love you can't let her down, come on and let

her enjoy herself while she can, I'll be fine and Timmy
and Xavier are both here in bed. It will do you good to be away from things too, so for me please love, go.' He went reluctantly but then was ringing every ten minutes. I told him I was going to bed so not to ring until I rang him later. God love him Noreen he is in an awful way. In one way it is good for me as I am so worried about him that I am not thinking about the other thing but then in another way I am thinking how will he cope if things turn out bad. He has always been so strong and even when we had bad times I was never afraid as I was sure he would sort it all out. Then again it is early days and he is in shock and I suppose neither one of us has really started to take it in.

When they left I got a headache and the doctor had given me strong painkillers and when I took two they made me feel lovely and peaceful and calm and drowsy. I fell asleep on the couch in the sun-room and did not wake till Xavier rang down for his breakfast at 3. Himself and Timmy then came down and we had a fry-up although I could not eat much, my appetite is up and down, I either want loads or none. Xavier then decided that the three of us should go into town shopping. He was pretty put out when I said I did not feel like it, I always love shopping with anyone but especially with Xavier and Timmy. Today, though I just didn't feel up to it.

I gave Xavier a few euro and they both went off to town shopping and I tidied up a bit and did the ironing and then fell asleep on the couch again.

The consultant's office rang this afternoon and woke me up. We are going to see him next week to arrange things. After the call I looked on the internet to read about other peoples' experiences of tumours and how they dealt with it. The first one I read was about a man who was diagnosed in 1970's. It was inoperable and there was no chemo then so he had to have radiation. However, he said that he felt that thinking positively and dealing with things with humour and laughter had helped as much as the medical treatment. He went on to have five kids and is still doing fine today. Isn't that a great story Noreen, it gives you hope and I am going to follow his example and use humour and laughter to deal with this. I am going to fight this now and expect to get better, not expect the worst.

I have not written to the kids for days. They will think something is up or that I am sulking for some reason. I'd better drop them a quick line now.
Love Áine

To: Deirdre@aol.com
Cc: Pearse@hotmail.com ; Kay@hotmail.com;
From: Mammy@ eirecom.ie
Nov 5th

Dear Deirdre, Pearse and Kay in no particular order
How are you all? I have been very busy over the last few days doing stuff. You know stuff like housework and going places and other things that women with a husband and her own children, her sister-in-laws only child and grandchildren have to do. So I'm busy, busy, busy.

Daddy and Marie are gone off to Dublin, they are staying overnight, I just rang them. Marie has bought a whole new winter wardrobe. Well Daddy paid, Marie chose the clothes. They are going out to some indie gig tonight, Daddy is delighted – not. It's his own fault, he'd had a few too many pints last week and promised Maire that they would spend a day or two doing exactly what she wanted. She said he was always asking her questions so he should come and see for himself and now he is.

Mrs D is getting on grand in New York although I am sure you know that Kay, Tina would have told you. I'm glad to say that Tina is doing a bit better now that her Mammy is there. I hope one day when one of you are pregnant or your future wife Pearse that I will be able to come to you to offer you support and the benefit of my experiences.

Make sure you don't all get pregnant together or I would not know where to go.

Xavier and Timmy are gone shopping for games for one of the consoles although I suppose they will buy clothes too. Timmy loves clothes shopping now that he is nice-looking.

Deirdre you being the caring person you are asked about the last test I was having, I have not had it yet but am going to the doctor next week so I will let you know what is going on when I know. I am delighted that you are going for the new job. You are a great teacher and any school would be glad to have you. Still though prepare well for the interview, the English are good at interviews, not very good at the job. You will do fine at the interview and you do have two weeks to brush up on things you know already. As I am saying this now I will also say that I am very proud of all of you, you are all doing fine jobs and settled in very well in your new homes. You are all children to be proud of and although sometimes I may seem to be cross or pushy it is only because I want you all to do better each day than you did the day before. Also I want you to know if you have any problems Daddy and I are here for you, no matter what kind of troubles you might have we are here, remember that. You are all loved very much.
Love Mammy

To: Mrs D@gmail.com
From: Mammy@ eirecom.ie
Nov 6th

Hello Noreen
First of all I want to tell you thanks so much for being there for me. I know you are busy enough with Tina in New York and I don't want to take anything away from your time with her but I know you well enough to know that you would tell me if you felt that I was. I also know that you would never not be there for me at a time like this as I would be there for you. I would love to be all noble and say 'but Tina comes first so I will stop writing' but I just don't feel that is something I can do in this situation and I know you would feel awful if I made the offer anyway. Especially if the treatment does not work and I die. See there is a bit of emotional blackmail there now for you which I am not below using but not on you, you know me way too well for any of my tricks, in fact you taught me some of them.

John and Marie are on their way home from Dublin now. John sounded a bit calmer so I'm hoping that it did him good. Marie said they had a fab time and they are going again before Xmas maybe even on Daddy's next job. John coughed wildly in the background which means 'don't hold your breath on that one Marie'.

I emailed the kids last night and said that I was going back to the doctor next week and I would let them know more when I knew more myself. I have been looking on line to see what other people in my situation did and to my surprise many of them did not tell their families right away which made me feel better about my own decision. It's not that I was looking for approval, I will go my own way, but I did want some confirmation that what I am doing is ok and that I have not got it completely wrong. You can never be sure of course but the way I look at it is if I had told them immediately by now they would be worn out with worry. They would be here actually and what would they be doing here. I'm not sick at the moment and I would be stressed worrying about them taking time off work. After all they may need to take time off again in a few weeks and they are all booked for coming home for Xmas anyway. I know that Deirdre and Omar are going away to Paris for the weekend; that would not happen if I had told them. Pearse is in some surfing gala next week; he could not do that if he knew. Kay has some exam coming up that she has been studying for months for, why should she miss that when there is nothing that she could be doing here. You see what I mean Noreen I just want them to carry on with their normal lives as long as they can.

The internet is great for giving information but you need to be careful as a brain tumour is such an individual thing. Still there is a lot of success and one site, brainsurgery.com says *Diagnostic accuracy allows the surgeon to work precisely where he or she wants to work with amazing efficiency and reliability, each and every time. The result is that the surgical incision has been reduced to an absolute minimum. Smaller incisions, less tissue trauma, and better surgical planning have reduced the risk of brain surgery from almost 90% in the 1940's to about 2% in the 1990's.*

That is very encouraging. All the sites say that some people come out of hospital two days after surgery. I will be one of them.

Well Noreen I can hear a taxi pulling up outside so they must be back. I'll write again later.

Love Áine

To: Mrs D@gmail.com
From: Mammy@ eirecom.ie
Nov 8th

Dear Noreen

I want to say that I must be driving you mad with all these emails. To be honest you don't even have to read them if you like although you did say to keep you informed on an hour-to-hour basis. You should thank God I did not take that literally I could as you know. Anyway as I was saying you don't have to read them all, I think the writing, the feeling of sharing is a great help to me so thanks for that.

I had a bit of a shock earlier, I decided to sit down and write a letter to John's parents, they don't have a computer, I asked Tony, John's brother. I wanted to ask them if they would be willing to try to sort things out with John, after all it's been years now since they stopped speaking to him because he married me, an orphan with no education or family or home. The disgrace of it all was too much for them. Well you know all that. The kids never understood why it was always one of their aunts or uncles who took them to see their grandparents. John wanted to tell them the truth but I thought it better to just say we were not talking to them. The kids got used to it, kids usually do. Anyway when I sat down I just could not write, I could not hold the pen or something, I

279

don't know I just could not write. I was really upset as it must have something to do with the tumour. I rang the doctor and he said he had been reading up on brain tumours and he said that there are studies into how different functions of the brain, including handwriting are affected by accident or disease so while it may not be a very common effect it is a known effect. He said he had also read about telling family about having a tumour and that I was doing the right thing for myself by telling them when I was ready to do so, when I felt I had the information I needed. He was so nice to me, he usually is abrupt and flustered but not today and that made me sad. He is treating me differently even though I have not changed at all, not yet anyway.

When I came off the phone I sat down in the kitchen and just sobbed. Underneath it all I am so frightened about everything. If I have to have surgery what will I be like afterwards, I might never be myself again, I might become a burden to John and my family and friends and I would not want to live like that at all. I want to carry on with my life as it is now, I believe that life is the most valuable gift but I don't believe that people should have to live under any circumstances, no matter how bad the quality of their life is. I am scared about leaving John and my family and friends, I know I don't know where I will be going but I don't want to go yet, I want to see all my grandchildren growing up and I want John and I to get old together. I certainly would not want to be up in Heaven and see John happily married to somebody else because what would happen when he died? Who would he pick to spend eternity with me or her? I won't be entering into a polygamous marriage up in Heaven that is for sure.

Noreen I just want to be here for my children, not having a mother means living your life knowing always that something important is missing. Although I never knew quite what I was missing having never had the experience of being a daughter it has still been there and I wish now that I had a mother to be with me through this. It will be so much worse for my kids as they are used to me being there. I may get on their nerves sometimes but I am here when things get tough. The worst thing is that I feel so alone. I know I have good people who will support me through all this but I can't help but feel that I am alone in a sort of bubble cut off from everyone else as it is only me who knows how I feel and I feel lonely because wherever I am going I am going alone. I did not know how hard being lonely is, it makes you re-think things like getting close to people as in the end one of you will be gone and then you have all that grief to come. Perhaps we would be better off never getting close to anyone as then they can't leave you.

I know that sounds awful and I'm sure I don't really believe it but I am thinking all sorts of things at the moment.

Say a prayer for me Noreen please.
Love Áine

To: Mrs D@gmail.com
From: Mammy@ eirecom.ie
Nov 10th

Dear Noreen

I just want to let you know I am feeling better this morning. After I emailed you last I spoke to John. He has been a bit calmer but I could see he was on the edge. I told him I had emailed the kids and he still said he wanted to tell them immediately. I lost my temper with him then and said 'this is my bloody brain John, it does not affect you so while I still have a brain let me at least make my own decision about this. There is no point in telling them anything until I know what I am dealing with, why worry them, they will think the worst, it's human nature. When I do tell them I will explain why I decided to do it this way as I know they will be upset that I did not tell them immediately and I will also tell them your position on the whole thing. John, while I'm at it I also want to say that you have to stop crying. I know it is an awful shock but I need you to be strong for me. I know we don't know what's ahead of us but we have to face it head on. Crying won't make a difference and seeing you cry makes me feel like I am letting you down. Please try to be calmer.'

He sat there looking at me and then he said 'I'm sorry I just feel so lost, since the day we met if I thought about it at all I always thought that I would be the first to go, to die you know. Why

283

would I want to be here without you, I could not even imagine a life without you. We have been together, just us since we were 16 and because I had you I was able to live happily when my parents made me choose between you and them. Nothing mattered as long as I had you so how am I supposed to face a life without you now'. 'John' I said 'we don't know anything yet, I have been reading where people have brain surgery and are out of hospital after two days. That could be me, why should we have the most awful outcome, we might have the best. In any case John while I absolutely love what you said, I'm afraid that you will have to carry on, no matter what. You have a responsibility to our children. Imagine if they lost one of their parents and then lost the other to grief? No John that is not an option and I know you and know you will always do your best for our family. So while I accept that you have had a shock you need to man up now for me'. He hates that expression 'man up' especially when it is aimed at him. He got up and kissed me on the cheek and went upstairs He came down after a while and gave me a print-out with this on it, he got it from brainsurgery.com

One of the most beautiful ironies of all of this technology is that it allows the surgeon to minimize everything. It is now possible to do all of the following, in a more complete and accurate manner:
1. Shorten the time of operation. Operations that used to take 12 hours now routinely take 1 - 2 hours, with better results!

2. Spare the normal brain. In other words, the down side of brain surgery has been greatly reduced. "Exploratory" surgery no longer exists. The "music lessons" are almost always preserved. Patients rarely wake up with new neurologic problems.
3. Do a better job. Total removal of tumours and vascular lesions is now possible. With primary brain tumours, 90-99% removal is now really possible with preservation of surrounding eloquent brain. (This was only a dream in the past).
4. Improve patient outcome. Risks are reduced, and patients do much better. You don't need to be "wiped out" by brain surgery any more. It is not uncommon for patients to leave the hospital two days after their surgery. In other words, brain surgery does not have to be traumatic; furthermore, it is a most successful tool in the treatment of brain diseases.

This cheered him up a lot and cheered me up too. We spent a relatively normal few days, grocery shopping, housework and watching the tv although your mind can't help wandering.
Noreen give my love to Tina. It's great to hear that she is doing well. Thanks for keeping all this to yourself love.
Love Áine

To: Kay@hotmail.com
Cc: Deirdre@aol.com ; Pearse@hotmail.com
From: Mammy@ eirecom.ie
Nov 18th

Dear Kay

Thanks for your email. No nothing is wrong girl we
are just a bit busy. Daddy and I took the kids out
to Fota Wildlife Park and we had a lovely day.
Daddy made a picnic the night before but the two
of us had to eat it in the car outside Dino's while
Marie and kids had their food inside. Still it was
lovely and enjoyed by all. The boys are very
affectionate and were kissing and hugging us all
day, it was lovely. If one ran up to get a kiss the
others had to follow Daddy loved it and so did I
actually. They wanted to sleep at our house and
we were going to let them but we did not get back
till 8 and they were all asleep in the back of the
car by then so Daddy helped Paul to put them to
bed and we had a cup of tea and went home.

The next day then Daddy had to go to Dublin
for work so I went with him and we had a lovely
day. I was going to do a bit of shopping but
instead we walked around the city down O'Connell
Street we went into the General Post Office for a
look around and you can really feel the history
there. We went on the Trinity tour as Marie plans
to go there next year. Then we had a late lunch
and took a walk around the Garden of Memorial,
oh my Lord it is amazing did you know there are

286

representations of discarded bronze age weapons at the bottom of the pond there. The statue of 'The Children of Lir' is beyond description you have to see it yourself and you all should next time ye are here. Perhaps even take a trip up over Xmas. We got home well after nine so we went down to Danny Mac's for a couple of drinks and we met Mr Ahern down there, he was hanging drunk, he's a disgrace that man always drinking. Poor Mrs Ahern is a ruined woman she is ashamed. They had both taken the pledge when they were 16 and neither of them had ever even tasted alcohol. I blame herself, Mr Ahearn must have been dying for a drink for the past 40 years and there she is running up to get their new pledge badges. If he'd had a drink at 14 like the rest of us he would have been well used to it by now and not be drunk after a couple of pints every night. I've always encouraged Daddy to go out for a drink with the boys but that is just the way that I am.

Last night we went out for a meal with Marie and Adam. I was shocked that Marie agreed to come and when I mentioned it she said 'see what asking nicely can get you Mammy'. 'What do you mean?' said I. 'Usually you say we are all going for a meal on such a night, you wear this you wear that, so and so cannot come because of her haircut and rubbish like that, yesterday you said "would yourself and Adam like to come out for a meal tomorrow, wear whatever you like you always look lovely" and Mammy that made a big difference'.

We had a great night but Marie's comments made me think perhaps I can be a bit harsh with you all sometimes. I don't mean to be like that I only want to encourage you to do your best and I know that you all do that so I won't go on at you so much in future and I am proud of what you have all done and of course Daddy and I love you all too. That has never been nor will ever be in question.

Love Mammy

To: Mrs D@gmail.com
From: Mammy@ eirecom.ie
Nov 21st

Dear Noreen
We were on the phone for 4 hours last night did you realise that? Still Noreen as you know I do sometimes need to write things down and as we are going to the hospital tomorrow to talk about a biopsy that thing on my brain is at the front of my thoughts again. Not that it goes away but we have been doing a lot of things that I have neglected before. You know I was only interested in shopping and fashion and planning family nights out and such like but in the last few days I have been doing other things which I have really enjoyed too and when I am back on my feet I am definitely going to give equal time to both if not more time to the family stuff. After all you can only buy so much and who really cares if my dress is this season or last. John could not tell if a dress came from Primark or Prada and I think that his attitude is the right one. Don't worry Noreen I will still be there for our girl-time, you know I could never be a hippy type although I won't mock them anymore.

So while I have really had a good few days when I go to bed at night I can't help but think is it all too late. Am I only doing this because of the thing in my head. Then I think it does not matter why I am doing it as it has made me look at things differently and it is not too late as I mean to change things when all this is over.

Noreen I will let you know how we get on tomorrow. Say a prayer that things will be better than we expect. I am dreading it but it has to be done. John will be there with me anyway holding my hand through it all. It's only now I'm realising how lucky I am to have him, I suppose we are lucky to have each other although I have not been the ideal housewife except at dinner parties.
Love Áine

To: Mrs D@gmail.com
From: Mammy@ eirecom.ie
Nov 21st

Dear Noreen
Well we went today and the doctor said that
according to the scan the tumour is benign but as
he said before the only way to know for certain is
to have a biopsy. He asked what we had decided
whether or not to go ahead. I asked him what
would happen if we just left things as they were as
I had read that benign tumours were slow growing
and that sometimes they are best left alone. He
said that due to where the tumour is, and
proceeded to show us where (I may as well have
been looking at the planet Mars) it is located, they
could not be certain of anything and advised us or
me in fact to go ahead. I said I suppose we'd
better go ahead so. They booked me in there and
then for the operation on 2nd Dec. So almost two
weeks left to wait but two weeks to enjoy the
family and do things together too.
Dr Nolan rang when we got home to see how we
had got on. He said that it is a good sign that they
are not rushing me in for the surgery as that would
indicate that it was more urgent.

He said that did not meant that it is not very serious but that it was better than having to go in right away. So that is something, isn't it Noreen. Love Áine

To: Pearse@hotmail.com
Cc: Deirdre@aol.com ; Kay@hotmail.com;
From: Mammy@ eirecom.ie
Nov 21st

Dear Pearse

Thank you very much for your email. We are delighted that the surfing went so well and you had great fun although that part about you losing your swimming trunks was not so funny and you might want to consider next time whether or not your nakedness is something that you want to discuss with your mother and sisters.

Kay in answer to your question I have been to the doctor and I am going in for tests on the 2nd Dec. As it is a test I do not want any of you to come home. I will mangle any of you that do as I do not want ye to use up holiday time with Xmas around the corner. You all know how I feel about Xmas so if any of you give up time to come over here for a test I will not be happy. I think it expedient to wait until after the test at least. I may have to have more tests who knows? The test is to see why my blood level keeps dropping and I may have to have a transfusion if it goes any lower so nothing too sinister as you know I have had it all before and then the blood level returns to normal so it will probably be the same this time.

Everyone here is doing well. Marie is home a lot more and we have chats in the kitchen some evenings. The kids are here a lot more too, the baby girls are divine and all I can say is that I just love them, all of them not just the girls. The boys are a bit wild but all of you were wild so the apple does not fall far from the tree.

I might go and do a bit of Xmas shopping this week. I know it's early but at least I won't have to rush around at the last minute. If you have time you should all do the same.

Remember any trails or tribulations or joys or anything at all Daddy and I are here for you. You are all loved very much.

Love Mammy

To: Mrs D@gmail.com
From: Mammy@ eirecom.ie
Nov 24th

Dear Noreen
Our phone calls are overtaking our emailing but I
wanted to write a few things that I did not say on
the phone.

I have emailed the children and told them I am
going into hospital which is the truth. Then I told a
lie. I know if I did not say why I was going in they
would ask me so I said I was going in with my old
blood condition. It was all I could think of although
I know they will worry anyway at least they have
experience of this and it has had positive
outcomes in the past. Also they know how much I
love Xmas and I'd say none of them would dare be
responsible for spoiling it. So they are under
caution and I think they will agree with me. I know
I am trying to change how I write to them but this
is in a good cause. I know you disagree Noreen
but it is what I want. After all what if I have the test
and they decide to leave things as they are. All
that worrying they would have done would have
been for nothing at all. I will tell them the truth
afterwards when they are home at Xmas.

What I want to talk about Noreen is this
loneliness that I cannot seem to get away from. I
know I am surrounded by people who love me and
I thank God for that but still I feel alone, like a lost

soul. I am now on a journey that I have to take alone; nobody no matter how well-intentioned can come with me. I get these twinges over my eye and to the side of my head, they are not very painful but they are a reminder of where I am going and why I am different from everyone around me. I hate this, I would not wish it on anyone but why did it have to be me. You know I've always been scared of being alone because I was alone for so much of my life and now here I am again. Is this a sign are we all truly alone? I don't want to think that but I have had so many things going through my mind. The other day I was talking to Nora's mother and she was talking about her diabetes and I swear I wanted to say to her 'shut up bitch and tell me when you have a real problem'. Can you imagine I wanted to talk to here like some gangster or gangsta whichever way you spell it these days. Now I admit that I am no great counsellor and I prefer not to know people's personal stuff but normally I would think 'I'm glad I'm not you' and here I was almost asking her to swap with me. I then cut her off midway through her next sentence and said 'I have to go' and walked away. I would not normally encourage her but I would let her finish her sentence and then say 'Sorry lovey I have to run meeting Xavier, late already, you know how he worries' as I walked away.

I know you said I might not feel so alone if I told the others but it is not like that Noreen, I could tell the world and I am still on my own; back where I always was and where I have always known I would return to. You know I have always been frightened of being on my own. My nightmare has been somehow, being me, I would lose my family and I would be like that woman in the old Squeeze song where the old lady lives in a hovel with only cats for company. 'Labelled with Love' it's called. That is how I feel now like it is all over for me and I am missing my home and family although I am still here and so are they. Am I losing my mind has that thing grown and is now pressing on some part of my brain that controls my sanity? I don't know what is happening to me. I'm scared.
Love Áine

To: Mrs D@gmail.com
From: Mammy@ eirecom.ie
Nov 24th

Dear Noreen
You are truly a great friend. All the hours we
spend on the phone and 'chatting' on-line, wasn't
that a great thing Marie showed us, we are very hi-
tech.

　　Thanks so much for talking me through my
being alone thing. I won't lie and say it is all gone,
it's not but I did talk to John about it last night, as
you suggested, well insisted as you were going to
tell him if I did not. He was great about it all and
said to just feel like I feel and then get it out of the
way. If only it was so simple Noreen but at least
he knows now. I have heard him cry a few times
when he thinks I'm sleeping, it breaks my heart.
He is a good man and does not deserve this
worry.

　　Anyway to try to change the mood I have
booked 3 days away at Dingle for John and
myself. Flying to Kerry and back. It may seem a
bit mad but we always said we would go, just the
two of us when we were first married. We went
many times with the kids but now it's time for just
John and me. I wanted to do something special
as we don't really know when we could go again
but anyway at the very least the 25th of Nov can be
another special anniversary for us.

Noreen I have banned phones and all other means of contact. John will ring Marie each evening to check on them but that is it so don't be worrying about not hearing from me in fact take a break girl. You deserve it.
Love Áine

To: Kay@hotmail.com
Cc: Deirdre@aol.com ; Pearse@hotmail.com
From: Mammy@ eirecom.ie
Nov 29th

Dear Kay

Thanks for your email love. Yes Daddy and myself had a lovely time in Dingle. We went to see the house we used to stay in when you were all younger and it is now a luxury villa.

Remember when we used to stay there and the flush never worked on the toilet. We used to have to flush it with buckets of water. Every holiday they told us it was fixed and when we got there it wasn't. Daddy used to get very cross because he was in charge of filling the buckets of water.

Kay you have been very reassuring about my going into hospital. Thanks for that. I'm not too worried but you know hospital is not the best place to be still it has to be done and got over with.

Although I did say on the phone I want to congratulate you again on being first in the exam. Well done but we would have expected nothing less. You are all very intelligent and have always had good exam results. Except when Marie went in straight after a cider session and wrote Ireland is a f*cking fascist state in the middle of a maths paper. Luckily Sister Bernadette checked it before it went off and it was also lucky that Marie was not expelled from school. She is still mad for cider. Daddy found 18 empty cider bottles under her

300

bed. Herself and Adam and their pals do be drinking up there regularly.   Daddy said he was going to ground her. Ground her and her over 18, she would only be laughing at him. I told him leave her alone she's only young.

So then Kay, Deirdre and Pearse I will speak to you on the phone before I go into hospital but I won't email again as I have things to do and people to see.

As always we love you dearly. Look after yourselves and each other.

Love Mammy

To: Mrs D@gmail.com
From: Mammy@ eirecom.ie
Dec 1st

Dear Noreen

I thought I would write before I went to bed as I probably won't sleep now. John is still up watching some sports programme or other. I'm not sure he will get much sleep either tonight.

So tomorrow is the big day. The biopsy day, at least it will be done by tomorrow night and who knows Noreen it could be the end of it all. I made the mistake yesterday of going on the internet and looking up what happens during the operation and it seems barbaric, drilling a hole in your skull and pulling out a piece of your brain. I was hysterical (I should have stuck with my decision not wanting to know medical stuff) and I was in the house on my own. For some reason I rang the priest. Now you know I'm not the best Catholic in the world or probably even in the house but I told him what was happening and within 10 minutes he was knocking on the door. We had a good talk and it helped as his father had gone through something similar but his was malignant. The priest was driving off just as John and Timmy came in and John thought the priest was asking for money and was prepared to chase him and give him a piece of his mind but he calmed down then when I told him why the priest was there.

Xavier and Marie know I am going into hospital but Marie and Adam are going to London tomorrow for a few days. They are staying with Deirdre and Omar and going to the o2 Arena to see somebody or other. Xavier, as you know, has a phobia of hospitals since he managed to get locked in the morgue one night and is apologising profusely for the fact that he won't be able to visit me. It suits me fine. John will put Timmy off and I told Paul and Nora not to come as I would be out the next day. I know I won't be out the next day but they would have to arrange babysitters so it would be difficult for them to come to the hospital without major planning. John will stay with me as long as they allow him to.

We had a lovely day today. We always buy the children Advent calendars and usually John would drop them off but I went with him early this evening and it was so lovely to see how much the calendars mean to them. They were so excited and Eoin said 'it's time to be good now, Santa will be here very soon so all the messing has to stop boys, those girls are good anyway so Santa will come to them for sure. Mammy we're all going to bed now cause we are good boys' 'Not yet' said Nora 'it's only half past five.' I was glad they did not go to bed as there was lots of time for hugs and kisses, and I was not even worried if they would spoil my clothes or make-up. Imagine I missed this all the other years and I'm not even sure why now as what could be more important?

So Noreen I don't want to drag this out but I want to say that I love you very much, you are a very important part of my family, my only sister and blood could not make us any closer. Thanks for everything Noreen and I will speak to you in a few days.
Love Áine

To: Deirdre@aol.com
Cc: Pearse@hotmail.com ; Kay@hotmail.com;
From: Mammy@ eirecom.ie
Dec 8th

Dear Children

I am home from the hospital and we will have the results in 7 to 10 days. The hospital will ring and let us know when to come. As you know I got out of hospital on the 5th but am feeling a little tired so not writing a lot.

Are you all prepared for Xmas? We are and I was delighted when I got home from hospital and Daddy and Xavier and Timmy had put up the tree and all the lights and decorations. I know usually that I do not allow anyone to have anything to do with the tree or lights or decoration but I must say that it was a lovely surprise although I may need to tidy it up tomorrow.

Daddy is cooking dinner at the moment. It will take me forever to clean the kitchen. Still it's a nice thought.

Eoin fed the babies with the chocolate from the Advent Calendars. They were both sick with vomiting and diarrhoea after all the chocolate. He is grounded now and not allowed to play his football match at the weekend.

He is heartbroken and has been phoning Daddy to ask him if he can get Paul to change his mind.

I hope Paul does, Eoin is the star player.
Love you all very much.
Love Mammy

To: Mrs D@gmail.com
From: Mammy@ eirecom.ie
Dec 9th

Dear Noreen

Well it is done. I can't tell you how happy I was to wake up and know where I was and who I was. I was in the ICU and I remember a man talking to me saying things had gone great. I was asleep for hours after. There was very little pain but of course I was on all kinds of medication. When I saw John walking into the ward for the first time after they let him come in I was just filled with relief that I knew him and even managed 'Hello John.' I stayed in for 3 days and came home on the 5th. I am still quite tired but that is to do with the anaesthetic too. Apart from that I feel same as always. We still have to get the results though. I really am hoping that I won't have to have any more surgery. I was talking to a nurse on the ward and she said often patients with benign tumours don't have to have further surgery. They monitor how the tumour is growing and if it's changing and things like that. She said many, many patients never had to have further surgery and live perfectly normal lives. That is very encouraging. We are going for the results on Monday so I will let you know when we know.

Say hello to Tina for me. I am delighted she is doing so well and as you know every day the baby gets a little bit stronger so I am sure she won't lose it this time Noreen.
Love Áine

To: Kay@hotmail.com
Cc: Deirdre@aol.com ; Pearse@hotmail.com
From: Daddy@ eirecom.ie
Dec 11th

Dear All

I think you might want to sit down to read this. I can only say it as it is there is no way of dressing it up. As you know Mammy was in hospital earlier in the month for a test. The test was nothing to do with her blood it was in fact a biopsy for a brain tumour which was discovered by an MRI scan. I know this is a shock and Mammy did what she did to protect you all. She will explain it to you herself but I don't want any recriminations as although I did not agree with her not telling you I admire her reasoning for not doing so. The reason that I am telling you now is that we went back for the result of the biopsy today and Mammy will have to have further surgery. Now it is important that you read this carefully; Mammy has a <u>Meningioma.</u> This is a benign tumour and it has a cure possibility of 80%. So that is a very good outlook. Mammy is fit and healthy otherwise and there is no reason why she would not be one of the 80%.

I think now it might be best if you could all come home as soon as you can, her operation is on the 19th Dec.

Daddy

To: Mrs D@gmail.com
From: Mammy@ eirecom.ie
Dec 11th

Dear Noreen

Áine asked me to let you know what happened today and said she will be in contact soon. She has a Meningioma. This is a benign tumour and it has a cure possibility of 80%. So that is a very good outlook. Áine is fit and healthy otherwise and there is no reason why she would not be one of the 80%. Unfortunately Noreen she is convinced that she will be one of the 20% who don't make it and I can't console her. Up to now she has been very good really, some bad days but really positive over all but this is too much for her. The family all know now. The surgery is scheduled for the 19th. Kay rang the hospital and has all the medical information and she will be here on 18th. Deirdre will be here on the 18th also and Pearse on the 17th. They have their own stuff to sort out as you know. Marie is devastated; asking me if her Mammy is going to die. Xavier is surprisingly composed and is sitting with Áine upstairs now telling her it will be alright.

Noreen I know I went off the head a bit when she was diagnosed but that is all over now and I will support her and I won't be breaking down in front of her under any circumstances.

Noreen I know she can be a bit contrary but I love her and if anything happens to her I don't know how I will cope, but I will cope as I promised her I would.

Something else has been preying on my mind too. As you know she told the children that her parents died in an accident and that is why she was an orphan. She did not want them to grow up pitying her or wondering, as she has always done herself, why she was not good enough. She did not want the children to know that her parents were married and had made plans to move to America before they knew about the pregnancy, apparently they did not find out until she was 7 months gone. They had both got good jobs and a baby was not in their plans for another 6 years. They decided to go ahead with their plans and handed her over to Social Services and obviously never looked back. She has known all this since she read her file when she was 7. The thing I'm wondering now is should I tell the kids the truth and try to find her parents. She said she would never search for them but things are different now. What would you think Noreen? Although I think I know what you will say 'leave it alone and deal with what is happening now' and you are right. I just answered the question myself.

I want to do the best for her and trying to contact people she does not know and she might not want to know would just bring more stress now when that is the last thing she needs.

I just want to tell you thanks for being there for her not just now but always.

Best wishes

John

To: Deirdre@aol.com
Cc: Pearse@hotmail.com ; Kay@hotmail.com;
Xavier@eirecom; Paul@gmail.com;
Marie@gmail.com
From: Mammy@ eirecom.ie
Dec 14th

Dear Xavier, Kay, Paul, Pearse, Deirdre and Marie
I am writing this to all of you as sometimes I think I can explain things better when I write it down. I was going to send you all individual letters but that feels too much like saying goodbye and I have no plans for saying that any time soon. In any case I found recently that am having problems actually writing so typing is the best I can do for now.

Daddy has told you all about the brain tumour and much as I wish I did not have it, I do. I would have told you all myself earlier but I was hoping that when I had the biopsy I would be told that no further surgery was needed especially as I did not feel sick at all. So I decided not to say anything about it until I knew what I was dealing with. I think the best way to explain why I decided to do what I did is to relay to you the conversation that I had with the doctor on the day we got the results of the MRI. He asked me when I was going to tell you all and I said to him 'if you were the person who was going to be told one of your parents had a tumour would you like to know as soon as they were told or would you like to carry on with your normal life for just a little while longer?' 'You know we keep surprises secret for as long as we can, even though that is good news we are giving to each other but we are in such a rush to tell bad news, I think it should be the other way round, keep the bad news to yourself as long as is possible and give the good immediately.' I was very sure that was the way that I wanted to go but I did look into it on the internet and I was certainly not alone in my thinking. I'm not trying to justify anything; I think I did the right thing. Daddy was not on my side on this issue but it was my choice. I love you all very much, each one of you as much as the other and I am proud of you and of all your choices too even if sometimes I did not agree with them. So although you may not have approved of my choice I wanted to keep the terror of it all away from you for as long as possible. I hope you will all understand my reasoning. As it turns out I have a Meningioma and the medical team think it best to remove it as these types of tumours can invade the bone or muscle. I may have to have radiation therapy after surgery but I won't know that until later. Hopefully there won't be any complications but I will probably have to take anti-seizure medication after which will be discontinued if I do not have seizures. There can be other complications but I want to concentrate on being well not on complications. If any complications do occur we will deal with them then.

Daddy said you are all coming home a few days earlier and thanks for that. I am looking forward to seeing you and it will give me such comfort to know you are there when I go down for the operation.

You know somebody mentioned to me that some of my emails may have been hurtful or upsetting to one or all of you. I want you to understand that I meant no harm. I was stupid sometimes I will admit, although I did not know it at the time, I was resentful of you going away to your great jobs but that was more to do with me than with you, I promise you that. A lot of it was that I would miss each of you so much and I wanted to keep you all close to me. I realise now that I can't keep you children forever and I am really proud of all of you and it's great to see you doing so well and let's be honest your successes have given me great bragging rights and I've spent many happy nights telling anyone who would listen how great you all are. I may not be the best at showing emotions but we all have things we can work on. Once I'm better I will visit you all regularly instead of always expecting you to come here and who knows perhaps one day we might all spend Xmas in New York or Sydney!

The next few weeks will be difficult for us all but we will get through things together whether we are all in the same country or not. It is a shame that it's happening over Xmas but for all we know I could be home by Xmas day. No matter what happens I know you will all be there for Daddy. I might complain about him sometimes but he is a great father and husband so remember that. I won't worry I know you all love him and get along with him and I know he won't be going through this alone.

So for the three of you who are away I will see you in a few days and for those of you at home I'll see you when I wake up if you are around.
Love you always
Love Mammy

To: Deirdre@aol.com
Cc: Pearse@hotmail.com ; Kay@hotmail.com;
From: Mammy@ eirecom.ie
Dec 16th

Dear All

Just to let you know things are going on as normal here. Xavier started work as a holiday postman yesterday morning. Timmy picked him up from the nightclub and took him to collect the post. Timmy said Xavier was so drunk that there was no way he could deliver the post so it's out in the boot of Timmy's car now. If the car was robbed with the post in it there would be a lot of trouble. I don't know why Timmy did not bring Xavier home and then deliver the post himself, he didn't have to go to work till 8.

Daddy called Xavier at 3.30 this morning to go to work but when Daddy got in later at 8.30 Xavier had not moved so there was no post delivered today either. Daddy and Timmy had been out delivering the mail from yesterday. The post office rang to ask where Xavier was and Timmy said they had a wrong number. Daddy was very cross with Xavier and then Xavier was very upset until I said I was sick and needed calm. They all looked guilty then but they did apologise and settle down.

I knew there would be trouble when Xavier was given that job. Early mornings and Xavier do not mix that is one of the reasons he has never had a job. All the interviews for jobs he would like are held early in the morning.

I'm fine and all the fuss with the post just goes to show that things go on as normal and I am grateful for that.

Love Mammy

To: Mrs D@gmail.com
From: Mammy@ eirecom.ie
Dec 16th

Dear Noreen
Although we spoke for hours last night I did want to say that I don't want you to worry too much about the operation. I'm certain that I will be fine and hoping to be at home for Xmas day all being well and there is no reason why things would not be well. As I said I was distraught when I found I had to have the second surgery but there is no point in thinking like that so now I am hoping for the best. Even so Noreen I do want you to pray for me.

I really don't have much more to say just that I love you and hopefully will speak to you soon.
Love Áine

To: Kay@hotmail.com
Cc: Deirdre@aol.com ; Pearse@hotmail.com
From: Mammy@ eirecom.ie
Dec 16th

Dear All

The postal saga is at an end. This morning Timmy went to pick Xavier up from the club again but when Xavier went to pick up the post from the sorting office he hurt his back and could not carry the bags and remember he had several bags from yesterday as well. Timmy rang me and said if we did not do something that Xavier could get in trouble for postal offences. Although a lot of this was his own fault I wouldn't let Xavier get in trouble; imagine if he went to prison, it doesn't bear thinking about, a beautiful boy like him. As Xavier was very drunk anyway I told Timmy to bring him home and I would ask Marie and Adam to deliver the post and that Xavier could give them the money, they always need money for cider. Well it took them 8 hours and I'd say most of the letters went to the wrong houses because they were drinking cider and dancing to Lady Gaga on the way round. Then they are both afraid of dogs so would not go in any house where a dog was so I said that they should put the letters for people with dogs back in the post box on the end of the street. Before all this I never realized how problematic it was being a postman. You see them there on their bikes looking tanned and handsome little realizing the problems that are involved. Marie and Adam were exhausted by the time they got home.

They said that there is no way that they would do tomorrow's round so I phoned the doctor and myself and Xavier went down. We told him about Xavier's back and the weight of the postbags. The doctor was a locum and gave Xavier a sick note saying he was in no fit state to carry heavy goods and that he could not work until after Xmas. Shur that's all worked out fine now as the job finishes on the 24th. Xavier will take the note down to the sorting office in the morning and collect the two days wages.

I'm doing fine and will see you all over the next couple of days. Loads of love to all of you as always.

Love Mammy

To: Daddy@eirecom.ie
From: Mammy@ eirecom.ie
Dec 18th

Dear John

It is very late and I know you are asleep so you won't open this until you get back from the hospital.

I want to say thanks for everything John we have had many happy years together and I know that there are many more to come. We have had our ups and downs especially in the early years when I was always scared you would leave me and I tested that theory to the limit. I know that I have not always been easy to live with, but you stayed there at my side through thick and thin and I will always stay by your side too.

I would be lying if I said that I'm not scared John. I am but I feel easier knowing you are there. I want to say that I love you very much and that it's that love that will see us through tomorrow. I will be fine tomorrow. I will be fine because I could never leave you.

So you sleep now my love and it won't be long till we are home together again.
Love Áine

To: Mrs D@gmail.com
From: Daddy@ eirecom.ie

Dec 19th

Dear Noreen
Áine has had the operation and things have gone as well as they could have. Obviously she is still in ICU but at least the operation is over with. She has been really brave throughout this although I know she was terrified. Hopefully now she will make a full recovery and will soon be back to her old self.

I cannot tell you how relieved I am that the operation is over with because once the operation is over with then it is on to recovery and that is what we all want.

She has no idea you are coming so it will be a great surprise when she sees you tomorrow. I will pick you up as arranged.
Best Wishes
John

To: Mrs.D@gmail.com
From: Mammy@ eirecom.ie

Dec 31st

Dear Noreen
Here I am at home and up and about again. I feel
fairly well considering but get a bit tired from the
meds which will be reviewed when I go back to the
hospital. Everyone has been marvellous and I'm
so happy that it's all over now. I'm sure that this
will be the end of it now. We know they got all the
disease so it should just be recovering now and to
be honest I feel like I'm nearly there already.

I want to say thank you so much for coming to
visit me Noreen, it was a great thing that you did
and you will never know how much it meant to me.
Once all the follow-ups with the hospital are
finished John and me are thinking of going to New
York so hopefully I'll be able to visit you and Tina
then. I'm thrilled that the pregnancy is going so
well. Imagine you'll be a Nana soon. I've seen
the grandchildren all over the holidays but they
have the house wrecked.

Noreen, don't mention this now but I think Nora
might be expecting again. Now I'm not sure but
Paul and herself were acting very shady when I
made the suggestion that she should have her
tubes tied yesterday. I can say anything I like now
as they can hardly be cross with a sick woman. I

324

hope to God now she is not. Paul is worn out already and hardly has time to go for a pint with the lads of an evening. I don't know what the answer is. I asked them if they knew there was a pill she could take but she got a bit huffy and went out for a smoke, which she has taken up recently. Paul looked very cross with her because he said to me 'I think you should get some rest now' and followed her out and when I looked out the window he was smoking too which was quite a shock to me. Still it's their own lives and you know me I wouldn't interfere.

Well Noreen I'll leave it there for now. I'm looking forward to a better year. So Happy New Year to you and yours and speak soon.
Love

THE END